I began to shrink. But it was strange, because as I shrank and my outer clothing slithered off me, I didn't feel like I was getting smaller. I felt more like I was getting stronger . . .

It was like I was made out of liquid steel . . .

Suddenly I sensed something over my head, a shape, a shadow, a figure. Lightning quick, I turned my head. My ears flattened back against my skull. The hair on my back stood up and my tail puffed out to three times its normal size. My claws extended. I drew back my mouth and showed my teeth.

It all happened in a split second. I was ready for battle.

> **Even the book morphs!**
> **Flip the pages**
> **and check it out!**

Look for other ANIMORPHS titles
by K.A. Applegate:

ANIMORPHS

The Visitor

K.A. Applegate

Scholastic Children's Books,
Commonwealth House, 1 – 19 New Oxford Street, London WC1A 1NU, UK
a division of Scholastic Ltd
London ~ New York ~ Toronto ~ Sydney ~ Auckland

First published in the USA by Scholastic Inc., 1996
First published in the UK by Scholastic Ltd, 1997

ISBN 0 590 19353 8

Printed by Cox & Wyman Ltd, Reading, Berks.

10 9 8 7 6 5 4 3 2

For Michael

Chapter 1

My name is Rachel. I won't tell you my last name. None of us will ever tell you our last names. Whenever I do use a last name, it's a fake. Sorry, but that's the way it has to be. And we won't tell you the name of our town, or our school, or even what state we are in. If I told you my last name, the Yeerks would be able to find my friends and me. And if they ever find us, it will be the end.

They might kill us. Or worse.

Yes, there really is something worse than death. I've seen it. I've heard the cries of despair from those doomed to be slaves of the Yeerks. I've watched as the evil grey slugs writhe and squeeze in through the ear and take over what

1

was a free human being.

There are five of us. Just five: Jake, Cassie, Marco, Tobias, and me. Marco came up with a name for us, for what we are now. He called us *Animorphs*. I guess that's as good a name as any for what we are. Mostly, I still just feel like a normal kid, you know? But I guess normal kids don't turn into elephants or bald eagles. And normal kids don't spend their free time fighting to save the world from the nightmares called Yeerks.

That day, the sun was bright. It warmed the earth below us. Warm air rose in an invisible bubble, a thermal. The thermal pushed up beneath our wings and we circled higher and higher and higher, till it almost seemed we could touch space.

Somewhere up there in cold space, up in orbit, was the Yeerk mother ship. Perhaps right over our heads.

The Yeerks were parasites. In their natural state they were just big slugs who lived in a sludgy pond called a Yeerk pool. But the Yeerks have the power to take over other bodies. They have enslaved many races throughout the galaxy — the Taxxons, the Hork-Bajir, and others. And now they had come to Earth, looking for more bodies to control.

Who was there to try and stop them? Well, off in space, there were the Andalites. But then the

Andalites were far away, and it would take them a long time to come to rescue the people of Earth.

On Earth, no one knew of the Yeerks. No one but five kids who were having fun being birds and riding the thermals.

I looked over at my friends. Some were a little way below, some were higher up. Jake was flapping his wings a little more than the rest of us. He had adopted a falcon morph. Falcons don't soar quite as well as hawks or eagles.

Tobias was the smoothest flyer. That was partly because red-tailed hawks are natural acrobats. Partly it was because Tobias had much more practice flying than the rest of us.

Too much practice.

<OK, Tobias, you were right. This is the coolest thing in the world,> I said.

<Want to try a dive? It's amazing,> he said.

I wasn't exactly sure that I wanted to dive, but what could I say? I don't usually turn down a challenge. So I said, <Sure.>

<Follow me.>

Tobias bent his wings back and plummeted towards the ground like a bullet.

I tucked my wings back and went after him.

The ground came rushing up at me.

I was falling! Falling, with nothing at all to stop me from splatting right into the ground!

It was like a nightmare.

3

We were going like ninety kilometres an hour, as fast as a speeding car. Ninety kilometres an hour, aiming right for the ground.

But even though it was scary, it was also way cool.

Forget surfing. Forget skateboarding. Forget snowboarding. You haven't had a thrill till you've ridden the thermals a few kilometres into the air and then gone hurtling straight down at maximum speed.

Air streamed past, just like when you open the car window and you're going really fast. It was like being in the middle of a hurricane. The leading edge of my wings was battered and vibrating. I felt my tail making dozens of tiny adjustments, moving a single feather one way or the other to keep me pointed straight. But one wrong move and I could have tumbled end over end. At this speed, if I suddenly tumbled I feared I could break a wing. A broken wing this high up was a death sentence.

<Tobias! I just realized something.>

<What?>

<This isn't like being an elephant. If I got in trouble as an elephant I could morph back to my human body. But I'm a long way up. If I morphed back to my human body . . . > I didn't finish the sentence. But I suddenly had this vision of me,

the *real* me, Rachel, dropping down like a stone towards the hard ground below.

I guess Tobias could sense the fear that was building in me.

<Let the eagle do the flying,> Tobias advised. <Relax and let the eagle's mind do the thinking. She knows what she's doing.>

<I'm glad one of us does,> I said nervously. It's strange when you're in a morph. You have the animal's brain in with your own. Usually you can control that animal intelligence. But not always. And sometimes you have to learn to let go, to let the animal take charge.

I relaxed. Instantly the vibration lessened. I felt more stable. The eagle was in charge — and Tobias was right: the eagle knew how to fly.

Then, to my amazement, I saw something go zipping right past us, much faster than either me or Tobias. It was Jake. His peregrine falcon's smaller wings made it harder for him to float on the thermals. But those same wings made him unbelievably fast in diving. It was as if Tobias and I were standing still.

<*Yaaaaaah ha ha!*> Jake yelled in our heads.

I would have smiled, if I'd had a mouth. Jake is like me. He loves excitement and adventure and being a little crazy. Maybe we're so alike because we're cousins.

Also, we're both a little competitive, I guess. It bothered me that he was a faster diver than I was. Just like it bothered him that I could soar better. I guess that sounds ridiculous, huh?

Zzzziiinnnngggg!

Something went right by my head.

<You hear that?> Tobias asked.

<Yeah, I sure did,> I said. <What was it?>

<I don't know.>

Instinctively, I pulled up out of the dive, straining every muscle in my wings as I opened them, and felt the shock of wind resistance. It was like opening a parachute.

The rest followed my lead. We were still a thousand metres up, but much closer to the ground than we had been.

Zziiiinnnnngggg!

I felt something go right through my tail feathers.

<Hey, someone down there is shooting at us!> I said.

<I can see them,> Cassie said. She and Marco had joined up with us. They had both morphed the same osprey. It was hard to tell them apart because you can't really tell *where* thought-speech comes from. <Two guys, over in the woods. They have a rifle.>

<I can't believe this!> I was really mad. <I'm

an endangered species. I'm a bald eagle! What's the matter with those creeps?>

<He's getting ready to shoot again,> Marco reported. <I can see him taking aim.>

<As soon as you see the flash of the rifle, dodge hard right!> I yelled.

A normal eagle or hawk or falcon would not have been able to figure that out. But we weren't just raptors. We still had our human intelligence. There are times to let the animal take over. There are other times when that superior human intelligence comes in handy.

<There! They fired!> Jake yelled.

Instantly I turned a sharp right. The bullet went whizzing by harmlessly.

<You know what? I don't think I like those guys,> Tobias said.

Tobias has special reasons for disliking anyone who would shoot at a bird.

<Me neither,> I agreed. <I have an idea.>

I explained what I wanted to do and the five of us flew off, out of range of the shooters. When we were far enough away, we went into a steep dive, down, down, faster and faster towards the trees.

I thought I was scared, diving from high up. Now I was diving at lower altitude, aiming directly at the trees. This was a whole new level of terror. With my eagle's eyes I could see the bark on the trees. I could see *ants* on the bark of the trees. It was like those trees were right in front of us.

I hoped the eagle knew when to pull out of the dive. If I slammed into one of those trees at ninety kilometres an hour, I was Spam.

Then, at just the right split second, like a perfectly trained squadron of fighter jets, we opened our wings and swooshed into the trees.

Unbelievable!

<*Ah haaaah!*> I heard Marco yell. <I don't know if that was fun or just insane!>

It was like some video-game nightmare. We kept most of the speed from the dive and now we were zooming through the trees so fast that tree trunks were just a brown blur all around us.

Tree! Bank left.

Tree! Bank right.

Tree! Dozens of feathers made the slightest individual adjustments. Muscles in my wings trimmed the angle of attack a millimetre one way, a millimetre back.

Tree! Tree! Treetreetreetreetree!

<*Yaaaaaaaaah!*> I yelled, half from terror and half from the total, out-of-control thrill of it.

In and out. Around and through. Zoom. *ZOOM!*

Suddenly, there they were, just ahead in a clearing. Two teenage creeps sitting in the back of a pickup truck. One guy had a blond ponytail.

The other one wore a baseball cap. They were a hundred yards away, like being all the way down a football field, but my eagle eyes were so good I could count their eyelashes.

The guy with the ponytail had the rifle. The other guy was drinking a beer. They were still scanning the skies, looking for us.

Guess what, morons? I thought as we raced at them. We're not up *there* any more. We're right here . . .

In . . .

Your . . .

FACE!

Chapter 2

They didn't even have the time to look surprised before we struck.

As a bald eagle, I was the biggest of the five of us. I could carry the heaviest load.

I raked my talons forward.

I opened them wide.

"Tsseeeeeer!"

Tobias's hawk let loose an intimidating shriek.

My talons hit the gun barrel and closed on it.

Tobias slashed the ponytail guy's head with his own talons. Ponytail shouted in pain and surprise and loosened his grip on the rifle.

"Hey!" the second guy yelled.

Zoom! I was out of there with the rifle in my talons.

With the additional weight of the rifle, it was a struggle getting any altitude.

"That bird has your gun, Chester! And that other one stole my beer!"

I glanced over and saw Marco. At least I think it was Marco. He had the beer can in his talons, half-crumpled.

<They're way too young to be drinking,> Marco said in his most parent-like voice.

I heard the ponytail guy complaining down below. "That ain't right. It ain't right that no bird should take my rifle like that."

I caught a little breeze and gained just enough altitude to get above the trees. But I was having a hard time. My wings were beating the still, dead air of the woods and not getting very much lift. I scraped the top of a tall pine tree and emerged from the woods. Still flapping hard to carry the weight of the rifle, I made it out towards the beach, over the low cliffs at the water's edge.

The blessed thermals were there. They lifted me up, up and out over the water. I relaxed, letting the warm wind carry me higher.

I dropped the rifle about a kilometre out in the ocean. I figured any jerk who would shoot at a bald eagle didn't need a gun. Marco dropped the beer with amazing precision right into a rubbish bin. He looked as proud as he would have if he'd

just thrown the winning basket in the NBA cham-
pionship.

<It's been almost two hours,> Cassie warned
us as we lazily drifted back towards shore.

Two hours is the time limit. If you stay in a
morph for more than two hours, you're trapped.

Forever.

There's an old, run-down church no one uses
any more not far from the beach. It has a bell
tower, although the bell is gone. We flew there.
That's where we had started from. Our clothes
and shoes were still piled there.

Four pairs of shoes for the five of us.

Cassie, still in her osprey body, peered down
at her watch lying on the floor. <Good. An hour
and a half. We should try never to go over an hour
and a half.>

We began to morph back into our human
bodies.

Morphing takes concentration. When you're
going from human to animal, it's harder. You really have to focus. But going back to human is
easier.

I focused in on my human self. I formed a
picture of myself in my mind — tall, thin, with
blonde shoulder-length hair. I focused especially
hard on the hair, because I didn't like my last
haircut. It was uneven at the bottom. Not that it

mattered. I just wished I could do something about the hair when I morphed. Unfortunately, morphing doesn't work that way.

The changes began quickly. The feathers that covered me began to melt. They ran together like hot wax. In some places when my skin reappeared, it would have this beautiful feather pattern for a few seconds.

My yellow bill sucked back into my mouth to become white teeth. That part sort of itched. It made me want to grind my teeth a few times.

My lips grew out around my teeth. My eyes went from pale gold to my normal blue. My legs grew quite a bit, from about three inches to normal size.

I looked over at Jake and saw the same things happening to him. Let me just tell you — watching someone morph is not a pretty sight. It's the kind of thing that would give you screaming nightmares if you didn't know it was going to be all right.

When Cassie morphs, she always does it kind of artistically. Like when she changes into a horse, she does it so it doesn't look totally creepazoid — she has a natural talent for morphing. If there is such a thing. The rest of us just let it happen however it happens. The results can be disturbing.

I happened to see Marco at the moment where his hairy boy legs came shooting out of this little bird body and I yelped. "Yahh! Gross."

"Ay, nyew donk luk so good yourself, Rachel."

His mouth was morphing even as he spoke. So the first few words were garbled and the last were normal. I think what he said was "Hey, you don't look so good yourself, Rachel." He was probably right. I was glad I didn't have a mirror.

My tongue grew fat in my mouth. My eyesight became faded and dim. The eagle's mind evaporated, leaving me all alone in my head. My wings became arms. My talons became toes. The scaly yellow eagle legs became my own legs, only they were still all scaly at first.

"Nice look, chicken legs," Marco said. "Do those come in extra crispy, too?"

I smiled at him. "You're not one to talk, Marco." I pointed down at the floor. See, his legs had changed back, but he still had huge osprey talons instead of feet.

As my skin began to appear, so did my morphing outfit. Fortunately, after a few tries, we had all learned to morph some very minimal clothing. Usually nothing more than skintight workout clothes or leotards. Not enough to go walking around in, but enough to keep us all from dying of embarrassment when we morphed in front of each other.

I checked out my friends. They were mostly normal again, with just a few remaining hints that they'd been birds a minute earlier.

Jake is kind of a big guy, strong-looking, with brown hair and serious, dark eyes — although at the moment, his eyes were shining with excitement. Sometimes being in a morph just totally breaks you out. Jake was a lizard once, and he still hasn't got over the fact that he ate a live spider. But I guess he enjoyed being a falcon, because he was babbling on and on about how great it was.

"That was so absolute!" he said. "It's like now, being back in a human body, I feel like I'm handicapped or something. I feel like I'm glued to the ground."

"And blind," Cassie agreed. "Human eyes are so lame for seeing things far away."

She grinned and spread her wings. She had managed to keep her wings till the very end. Now she looked like some strange angel. Oddly, the look worked for her. The osprey's metre-wide, grey-and-white wings were incredibly cool.

"Do you think you could fly?" Jake asked her. He looked a little awestruck.

Cassie laughed. "No, Jake. This body weighs

about thirty-six kilos. These wings aren't built for that kind of weight."

She morphed her wings into arms in about three seconds and laughed gaily.

Marco shook his head. "Great. When *we* morph we look like some mad scientist's genetic experiment gone totally crazy. And Cassie gets to look like an angel."

Cassie and I have been friends for a long time, although to look at us, you wouldn't think we'd hang out together. Cassie is casual to the extreme. The girl just doesn't care about clothing or style. I swear she would wear overalls to a wedding if someone didn't stop her.

Cassie lives on a farm and her whole family is massively into animals. Her dad used the barn to run the Wildlife Rehabilitation Clinic, which is a kind of hospital for injured animals. It's always full of birds and skunks and opossums and coyotes and every other animal you can think of.

Cassie's mum is a vet, too. She works at The Gardens, this huge zoo and amusement park. So maybe Cassie was just born with an instinct for understanding animals. All I know is she's always finished morphing while the rest of us are still looking like creepy half-human, half-animal monsters.

As for me, well, it's not that I'm Miss Fashion or whatever, but I do like nice clothes. I guess that, plus the way I look, makes a lot of people think I'm stuck-up or something. People do think I'm pretty. But to me that's just an accident, you know? Looks are not the important thing. It's what's in your head that counts, and that's what I concentrate on.

Of course that's another area where Cassie and I are a little different. I guess she would say, "No, it's what's in your heart that counts." She's a natural peacemaker. If there's ever a hassle within the group, it's usually me and Marco that caused it, and Cassie who got us all calmed down.

"Personally, I'm glad to be back to my regular body," Marco said. "The flying part is great, but it's not a good idea to be able to see that well."

"Why?" Jake asked.

"Look, Jake, how many times have you been walking around the mall or whatever, and you'll see a girl who seems good-looking from far off, but when you get closer it turns out she's a skank? I mean, if you could see this well all the time — "

"Excuse me?" I interrupted. "I'm sure I didn't hear you say what I thought you just said."

"I wasn't being sexist," Marco protested. "It goes both ways. See, from far off, I look taller than I am."

Marco is a little self-conscious about being

17

short. He has long brown hair and a dark complexion, and most girls think he's really cute. But being small bothers him.

"Your problem isn't with people seeing you too well," I said. "It's with people hearing you too well. You *look* like a fairly smart guy. Then you open your mouth. . . ."

Marco just grinned. Marco lives to annoy people. He really is extremely smart and basically nice, underneath it all. It's just that the boy loves to provoke people.

Marco and Jake are best friends, even though Jake is serious and thoughtful and always trying to do what's right, while Marco is sarcastic and temperamental and is the most reluctant of the Animorphs. Marco still thinks we should just give up the battle against the Yeerks and try to stay alive. But with Marco you never know if he *really* believes that, or is just saying it to be contrary.

"Well, let's get out of here," Jake suggested. "I have homework to do."

"Me too," I said. "And I have gymnastics class this afternoon and I'm totally unprepared."

Cassie sighed. "It's such a drag. The chores and the homework all come rushing back as soon as we change back into our boring human selves."

As soon as she said it, Cassie bit her tongue. She cast a regretful look to Tobias.

See, while all of us had changed back, Tobias

had not. Tobias was still a hawk. Tobias, who had once had unruly blond hair and eyes that seemed hurt and tender and hopeful all at once.

Tobias had been trapped while trying to escape from the hellish nightmare of the Yeerk pool. He had stayed more than two hours in that morph.

We had all returned to our human forms, but Tobias was still a hawk.

Tobias will always be a hawk.

Chapter 3

We all walked most of the way home together, feeling worn out. The flying was a little tiring. And morphing always takes a lot out of you.

Tobias flew high overhead. He didn't really participate in the conversation. It's hard for him. See, he can think-speak to us and we can understand him, but when we're in human shape we can only talk in the normal way. He can't hear us unless he's close by, and he can't be close and still fly.

"This morphing thing would be so excellent if it weren't for the whole thing with the Yeerks," Marco was saying. "I mean, if it were just normal, we could really use these powers."

"To do what? Fight crime?" Jake asked.

Marco looked at him with a mixture of pity and amusement. "Fight crime? Who are you, Spiderman? I'm talking show business. Movies! TV shows! I could go on Letterman. I could be an entire episode of *Stupid Pet Tricks* all by myself."

"You're right," I said, batting my eyes so he would know I was kidding, "you already have the stupid part down."

"We'd be hot in horror movies," Cassie said.

"Or how about as stuntmen?" Jake suggested. "One of us could jump off the tallest building and it would be totally realistic. Then we just morph into a bird on the way down and fly away."

"Now I'm *really* mad at the Yeerks," Marco said. "They're getting in the way of my showbiz career. I could be a millionaire. I could be trading funny lines with Dave. I could have beautiful Hollywood supermodels all over me."

"Uh-huh," I said, with a wink at Cassie. "Lots of women love animals. But sooner or later you'd have to change back into your actual self, Marco. And then, boom, they'd be outta there."

We walked along the boulevard that goes by the construction site. It's this huge area of half-finished buildings with rusted earthmovers and cranes and backhoes scattered around. I guess it was originally going to be a shopping centre, but for some reason they never finished it.

We didn't take the usual shortcut *through* the

construction site, like we would have in the old days, though. See, it was at this construction site that we saw the Andalite prince's damaged fighter land. It was here that the Andalite warned us of the Yeerk conspiracy and gave us our special powers.

It was also here that we saw the Yeerk commander, Visser Three, murder the Andalite prince. Visser Three is the only one of the Yeerks who has our same power to morph. Visser Three is an Andalite-Controller, meaning he has an Andalite body. A human-Controller is a Yeerk with a human body. A Taxxon-Controller is a Yeerk with a Taxxon body. You get the idea.

Visser Three is the only Yeerk ever to capture an Andalite body. So he's also the only Yeerk who can morph.

That night at the construction site, he morphed into some creature from a far-off planet, a huge, horrible monster. And then he took the Andalite and . . .

You know what? I really don't want to talk about that. . . You'll have to ask Jake.

We all fell silent as we passed by the site. Then I noticed that Cassie had stopped walking and was just standing there. I went back to her and realized that she was crying.

"Are you OK?" I asked.

She shook her head. "No. Are you?"

I sighed. Flying around in the sky had been a wonderful distraction. But my head was still full of awful memories. "I guess not," I admitted. "Last night I had a terrible nightmare about the Yeerk pool. I was back down there. Down there in that vast open cave. And I was hearing the screams and cries of the people being dragged to the pool."

Cassie nodded. "You know what's worse than the screams? The way they stop screaming once the Yeerk is in their heads. Once they've become Controllers. Then you know they are slaves again. Lost."

"Like Tom."

We both turned. It was Jake. He and Marco had seen us stop and had come back.

Tom is Jake's brother. Tom is a human-Controller — a human being enslaved by a Yeerk in his head. We'd found the Yeerk pool and gone down into that hell to get Tom. We'd failed. We'd barely escaped with our lives.

Cassie put her arm around Jake's waist. "Someday we'll save Tom," she said.

Jake kind of stroked Cassie's head. I guess he got embarrassed, because he instantly pulled away. Cassie didn't mind. She knows how guys are about showing their true feelings.

I looked across the construction site and saw Tobias come fluttering down out of the sky. I couldn't see where he landed, because that part of the site is hidden from the road, but I knew right where he was — on the actual spot where the Andalite had died. Somehow, in those brief moments when the Andalite had been with us, Tobias had formed some kind of special bond with him.

We started walking again.

"We need to find another way to get at them," I said angrily. It bothered me, imagining Tobias back in that maze of never-finished buildings mourning for the Andalite.

"Get at who?" Marco asked suspiciously.

"The French, Marco," I said sarcastically. "Who do you think? The Yeerks, duh."

"Whoa, whoa, whoa!" Marco said. "We tried that, remember? We went down into the Yeerk pool after them and got our butts kicked. Yeerks ten, humans zero."

"So you figure you should just give up?" I demanded.

"We lost one game," Jake said. "You don't quit the sport just because you lose one game."

"Some game," Marco said bitterly. "Some sport."

"We didn't lose, anyway," I said. The others looked at me like I was crazy. "Look," I explained, "I know we didn't save Tom, and we sure didn't stop the Yeerks. But we gave them some reason to be afraid, at least."

"Yeah, they're terrified of us. Visser Three probably can't sleep at night, he's so worried about five kids," Marco said sarcastically. "Look, Visser Three doesn't think we're a threat. He thinks we're lunch."

"He doesn't know who — or what — we are," I pointed out. "The Yeerks are convinced that we're Andalite warriors because they know that we can morph. And they know that we found the Yeerk pool, and infiltrated it, and took out a few of their Taxxons and Hork-Bajir while we were at it. I think they're probably a little nervous, at least."

Jake nodded. "Rachel's right. But just the same, I don't think we want to try to go back to the Yeerk pool. Besides . . . the door is gone."

We all stopped and stared at him.

He shrugged. "Look, I just wanted to see if the door still worked, OK? Just in case. But it's not there any more."

The door leading down to the Yeerk pool had been hidden in the janitor's closet of our school. There were dozens of doors to the underground Yeerk pool, spread all over the city, but this was the only one we knew about.

"So we find another way to get at them," I said. "We can follow Tom again, when it's time for his Yeerk to return to the Yeerk pool." Yeerks have to go to the pool every three days. They drain out of their hosts' heads and soak up Kandrona rays.

"No. We leave Tom out of it," Jake said firmly. "If we call attention to him in any way, the Yeerks may decide he's trouble for them. They may just decide to kill him."

Marco gave me a sour look. "This is what you want to keep doing? Risking our lives and the lives of everyone we know? For what?"

"For freedom," Cassie said simply.

Marco didn't have a smart answer to that.

"There's still Chapman," Jake said.

Chapman is our assistant principal. He's also one of the most important human-Controllers. He runs The Sharing, the club that helps recruit unsuspecting kids into being hosts for the Yeerks.

"If there were some way for us to get close to Chapman . . ." Jake let the words hang in the air. He carefully didn't look at me. But I knew what he meant. He'd obviously been thinking about this for a while.

"Melissa?" I asked.

He nodded. "It's a possibility."

See, Melissa Chapman, Assistant Principal Chapman's daughter, is one of my closest friends. Or at least she used to be. The last few months, she'd been acting very strange towards me. Like she didn't care any more. We take gymnastics together. Actually, we got into it at the same time. You know — something to do together.

"I don't like using a friend that way," I said.

"Oh, suddenly the mighty Rachel is weaseling," Marco crowed. "You don't like using your friends? You're pretty willing to risk *my* life."

"Sure, Marco, but who said you were my friend?"

"Very funny," Marco said. But at the same time he looked a little hurt.

"Kidding, Marco," I said. "Just kidding. Of course you're my friend. But you're an Animorph. Melissa is just an innocent bystander."

"I wish I had never come up with that word," Marco said. "Animorph. Gimme a break."

"Rachel, Melissa's father is one of the main Controllers," Jake said gently, ignoring Marco. "She's in this whether she likes it or not."

I felt a bitter taste in my mouth. Jake was right, of course. Chapman was the logical lead to follow. And Melissa was our way to get close. It made sense. It made sense for me to betray an old friend.

It also made me feel like dirt.

27

Chapter 4

The next day after school I headed for my gymnastics class at the YMCA, which is just across from the mall. They have a big indoor pool, so the entire building always smells of chlorine. Except for the weight room, which just smells like sweat.

My class is taught in a smaller room, with blue mats covering the floor. We have balance beams and uneven parallel bars and a vaulting horse with a springboard.

I'm OK at vaulting and the parallel bars, but I'm pretty lame at the balance beam. To be honest with you, it kind of scares me. It takes such total concentration.

It's not one of those real serious gymnastics classes. I mean, none of us is going to be going to the Olympics. When I started out, I had dreams of being the next Shannon Miller. But then I started to grow. I'm pretty tall now, for my age. People look at me now and say, "Oh, you're going to be a model," not "Oh, you could be a gymnast."

Most of us in the class are too tall or too heavy to ever be serious gymnasts. We do it for fun and for exercise. I do it because I've always thought of myself as kind of clumsy. My mum says I'm not, but that's how I feel anyway.

Besides, it's just cool, hitting the little springboard and flipping through the air to bounce off the vaulting horse and stick the landing. Not as cool as flying, maybe, but fun just the same.

Melissa Chapman was in the locker room changing into her leotard when I came in. She's the exception to the rule in our class. She *does* look like a gymnast. She's small and thin, even though she doesn't starve herself like some fools who want to get into gymnastics. She has pale grey eyes and pale blonde hair and pale skin. She looks like one of those solemn elves in a Tolkien book. At first glance she looks delicate, but when you look a little closer, you see strength there, too.

Melissa gave me the kind of not-very-warm

smile she always gives me lately. Like she was distracted, or thinking about something more important.

"Hey, Melissa," I said. "How's it going?"

"Fine. How about you?"

"Oh, pretty much the same old thing." That was a lie, of course. But what was I going to say? Yeah, Melissa, same old same old. Been turning into animals and fighting aliens. You know, the usual.

Melissa didn't say anything else. She just adjusted her leotard and started to do a few little stretches. That's the way it was. We said hi, but not much more. It used to be we were very close. She was my second best friend, after Cassie.

"Melissa, I was thinking . . . maybe you'd like to walk over to the mall with me after class? I have to buy a new pair of trainers."

"The mall?" She stammered a little, and then started blushing. "You mean, go shopping?"

"Yeah. You know — walk around and look at stuff and check out the cute guys and diss the snotty women at the perfume counters."

I tried to sound casual, like it was no big deal. In the old days, it would have been totally nothing. But now Melissa looked like a trapped animal.

When had Melissa and I got to be such strangers?

"I'm, um, kind of busy," Melissa said.

"Oh. That's cool. I understand."

But I didn't understand. Not at all. She started to walk away. I was going to let it go, but then I remembered: this wasn't just about a friend who had drifted away. This was about her father, one of the leaders of the Controllers. One of our most dangerous enemies.

I grabbed her arm. "Melissa, look . . . I feel like we've kind of gone in different ways, you know? And I miss you."

She shrugged. "OK, well, maybe we could get together sometime."

"Not *sometime*, Melissa, that's just you blowing me off. What's going on with you?"

"What's going on with me?" she echoed. For a moment a look of extraordinary sadness darkened her eyes and tugged downward at the corners of her mouth. "Nothing is going on with me," she said. "We'd better get out there or Coach Ellway will have a fit."

She pulled her arm away.

I just watched her go. I felt like a complete and total jerk. Something had happened to Melissa. And I hadn't even noticed. She was my friend and something had changed in her, and I hadn't seen it. I'd just gone my own way.

And now I was only *acting* like a concerned friend. The truth was, I was only paying attention for my own reasons.

31

I wasn't able to concentrate on the lesson. Not concentrating when you're doing gymnastics can be painful. I slipped on the balance beam and banged my knee so badly I cried.

Melissa was the first one to rush over. And for about ten seconds she was the old Melissa. But by the time I'd got back up, she was off across the room in her own little world again.

It was right then that the terrible suspicion started.

Melissa had been acting very strangely. Her father was a Controller.

I looked at her from across the room and felt a chill.

Was she one, too? Was my old friend Melissa a Controller?

I didn't go shopping after my lesson. I didn't really feel like it. Melissa's eyes, the way she had looked at me, kind of killed my urge to shop.

I was supposed to head over to the mall, then call my mum when I was done to come pick me up. That was the plan. But since I didn't feel like mall-crawling I just headed home. Alone. With the sky growing dark as rain clouds moved in.

It was stupid and careless of me. But I guess I was preoccupied with other things. Although at least I had the sense to stay out of the construction site.

I was walking down the pavement that runs along the boulevard when suddenly I realized that a car had pulled up just a little way down the road from me. A guy got out. He looked like he was in high school or even college. He also looked like trouble.

I should have turned around and run back towards the mall. But sometimes I don't always do the sensible thing. Sometimes I regret not doing the sensible thing. This was one of those times.

"Hey, baby," he said. "Want to go for a little ride?"

I shook my head and clutched my gym bag close. What an idiot I was to be so careless!

"Now, don't be stuck-up, sweet thing," he said. "I think you'd better get in the car."

The way he said it didn't sound like an invitation. It sounded like an order. Now I was really afraid.

I clutched my gym bag close as I passed him.

"Don't ignore me," he hissed.

He reached for me and missed. I walked faster. He was behind me.

I broke into a run.

He ran after me.

"Hey. Hey, there! Come back here."

I had been stupid going out alone. But fortunately, unlike most people, I wasn't helpless.

As I ran, I focused on something completely

different. I concentrated on an image in my mind.

Then I felt the change begin. My legs grew thick. My arms grew big, bigger. I could feel myself growing large. Large and solid. I felt the squirmy sensation of my ears becoming thin and leathery.

But it wasn't enough to just look creepy. This guy had made me mad. I wanted to scare him half to death.

My nose suddenly began to sprout. Then, from my mouth, like two huge spears, the tusks began to appear.

I figured that was about enough. I broke my concentration, which stopped the morph.

I stopped suddenly. The creep barrelled right into me.

He was not going to like what he was about to see.

Chapter 5

I wanted to tell the jerk to step off. What I wanted to say to him was, "So, you still want to go for that ride?"

What I really said was "*HhhohhHEEEEERRR!*"

The guy stopped dead. He just stared.

What he saw was me, halfway through morphing into an African elephant. I had about a third of a trunk and most of my huge fanlike elephant ears. My legs were like stumps. My arms looked like Arnold Schwarzenegger's, only grey. And my tusks stuck about half a metre out of my mouth. Just to make things extra weird, I still had my normal hair and my normal eyes.

Suddenly, the guy wasn't interested in hassling me.

"AAAAAHHHHH!"

He turned. He ran. For a minute he forgot he even had a car. Then he turned around and jumped in through an open window.

He started the car and took off.

He was definitely breaking the speed limit as he tore out of there.

I concentrated again and began to reverse the morphing process, going back to human shape. I had been wearing a loose sweater and leggings, which was good. They had both stretched. But my shoes had been split open by the sudden growth of my elephant feet.

It had started raining, so the trip home was going to be very unpleasant. "Oh, great!" I muttered. "I have got to remember to kick off my shoes before I morph into an elephant."

Just then, a second car pulled up and came to a stop. The window rolled down.

"Hey, Rachel." It was Melissa. I recognized the voice. "Do you want a ride home?" She didn't sound very excited by the idea. I looked through the car window, past her.

Chapman was behind the wheel.

A wave of sick fear swept over me. Had he seen what I'd just done? If he had, then I was dead. My friends were dead.

"I'm . . . I'm fine," I said. "I could use the exercise."

"Nonsense, young lady," Chapman said, sounding like his usual assistant-principal self. "It's beginning to rain. Get in."

What was I supposed to do? I forced a smile. It wasn't easy. "Thanks," I said.

Melissa was in the front with her father. I sat in the back. I tried not to shiver. I tried not to stare at the back of Chapman's head. That's how it is when you're around a Controller. You know that evil slug is right there in the Controller's head, attached to all his nerve endings. Controlling the human brain. Dominating it.

It's hard not to stare when you think of what is squeezed inside that skull.

"When we were stuck back at the red light it looked like some guy was bothering you," Melissa said. "Then he ran off. Was he bothering you?"

"Um . . . no," I lied. "He was . . . he was just picking up something he dropped by the side of the road."

Pathetic! I was such a lame liar.

I saw Chapman's eyes watching me in the rearview mirror. He looked like normal old Chapman. That's the problem with Controllers. There is no outward clue. They look so normal.

"He went running off like the hounds of Hades were after him," Chapman said.

"Did he?" I said in a squeaky voice. "I wasn't

looking. I guess it was the rain. That's probably why he was running. There. You can turn left there."

"I know where you live," Chapman said.

I almost swallowed my tongue. Was that a threat? Did he suspect? Did he guess? Was he looking at me strangely?

Or was I just being paranoid?

He pulled up in front of my house. My heart was hammering, but I was determined to act casual. "Thanks for the ride, Mr Chapman," I said.

"Hey, Melissa, I was totally serious about us getting together, OK?"

She nodded. "Sure, Rachel. Absolutely."

I closed the car door behind me. I had escaped. I was alive. I'd probably just been imagining things.

Then I heard Melissa call out to me. "Hey. What happened to your shoes?"

I looked down. My shoes were in tatters, the result of my feet growing from a size six to a size three hundred in about five seconds flat.

"See?" I said, as lightly as I could. "I told you I needed to go shopping."

Melissa just looked puzzled. Her father stared at me with an expression I could not read.

I was shaking like a leaf when I walked into my house. I headed upstairs to my room and stuffed my ripped shoes into the bin. Only then did I go back downstairs and say hi to my mum. She was at the kitchen table, half hidden by a pile of buff-coloured books. My mother's a lawyer, and she brings work home a lot so she can be around me and my two little sisters. She and my dad are divorced. I only get to see my dad a few days a month, so mum feels guilty when she isn't there for us.

"Hi, honey," she said. Then she got her "suspicious mother" look. "How did you get home? You didn't walk, did you? You were supposed to call me."

"Melissa and her dad gave me a ride," I said. Well, it was the truth. Sort of.

She relaxed and made a point of closing her book. "Sorry. You know I worry about you."

"Where are Jordan and Sara?"

"They're in the family room watching another one of those scary shows. Of course, tonight Jordan will be sleeping with her night-light on and Sara will end up in my bed, no doubt. I don't know why they like things that frighten them. You were never that way."

It almost made me laugh. I felt like saying, well, Mum, I don't have to watch things that are scary, I *am* scary. Should have seen me a little while ago with tusks sticking out of my mouth and a metre-long nose.

What I really said was, "So, what's for dinner?"

My mother winced. "Pizza? Chinese? Anything else you can order over the phone? I'm sorry, but I have this brief and I have court in the morning."

"Mum," I told her for maybe the thousandth time, "I don't mind pizza. Sorry, but your cooking isn't all that great, so it's no big deal ordering pizza."

"Well, at least get some veggies on it," she said.

After dinner I called Jake.

"Do you want to come over?" I said. "I got that new CD, if you want to listen to it."

There was no CD, of course. It's just that we always have to be careful. Like I said, Jake's brother, Tom, is a Controller. He could be listening on the extension. Then I called Cassie and Marco and told them the same cover story.

When they arrived I told them about Melissa, and then I told them about my little run-in with the creep. I did not tell them about Chapman driving me home. I don't know why. But when I saw the way Marco exploded, I was glad I hadn't told them the whole story.

"Oh, that was dumb! Dumb! DUMB!" Marco said. "What if that guy is a Controller?"

"He wasn't a Controller," I said scornfully. "Why would the Yeerks want to make a Controller

40

out of a punk? They want people in positions of power."

"We don't know that for sure," Jake said. "Tom isn't in a position of power."

"And how about people driving by in their cars, or looking out of the windows of their homes?" Marco asked. "And what if he runs and tells someone about this girl who suddenly sprouted a trunk and tusks?"

"No one is going to believe a lowlife like that," I said.

"His friends won't believe him," Marco said poisonously, "but a Controller *would* believe him. A Controller would know what it meant."

Yes. A Controller would know what it meant. A Controller like Chapman. Or even Melissa, if she was one of them.

I felt sick. It was like my whole life was nothing but lies. Lies to Melissa. Lies to my mother. Now I was lying by not telling the others the whole truth.

"OK, I screwed up," I muttered.

"You sure did!" Marco crowed. "You screwed up so — "

"Marco, let it drop," Jake said. "Rachel knows she made a mistake. We all make mistakes."

Marco rolled his eyes.

Cassie gave me an encouraging smile. "It *was*

41

dumb putting yourself in that position, Rachel. You need to be more careful. But still, I'd have paid my next ten allowances to see the look on that guy's face."

"The important thing is that it doesn't sound like Rachel can use Melissa to get to Chapman," Jake said. "Not if she's a Controller herself. And not if she's going to continue being weird to Rachel."

"I guess we'll have to find another way," I said quickly. "I mean, we know where Chapman's office is. We know where his house is. Maybe we could just morph into some small animals and hide out."

"Small animals like what?" Marco asked. "When Jake turned into a lizard he got stepped on. He lost his tail. Besides, what are you going to morph into? A cockroach?"

We all shuddered at the thought. The smallest, strangest thing anyone had morphed so far was when Jake had done the lizard. It creeped him out big time. A roach would be even worse.

"The problem with being a cockroach," I said, "aside from the fact that it is too gross to believe, is that roach senses might not even be useful to us. Can a roach 'hear' in a way that would make it possible for us to understand *what* we're hearing?"

We all looked at Cassie. She's sort of our expert on animals.

Cassie held up her hands. "Oh, come on. Like I know how a cockroach sees and hears? We don't take care of roaches at the rehab clinic."

We all sat there feeling glum for a few minutes. But I wasn't going to let it drop. This was about more than just striking a blow at the Yeerks. I had to find out if Chapman suspected me. If he did, we were all in terrible danger.

I happened to glance over at my desk. There was my maths homework, still not done. That didn't make me feel any better. But then I looked at the photos I had mounted in one of those big frames with six different holes. One was of me with my mum and dad on a whitewater rafting trip we took. One was of me visiting my dad at his job — he's a weatherman on TV. We were grinning in front of a map of storms. Another picture was of Cassie and me riding horses side by side, with Cassie, as usual, looking like she'd spent her entire life in the saddle, and me looking like a total dweeb.

But the picture that got my attention was one taken a couple of years ago of Melissa and me.

I got up and went over to take the frame down. I stared hard at the picture.

"What?" Jake asked. "What is it?"

"It's me and Melissa," I said. "It was like her twelfth birthday, or some birthday, anyway, and we were out on her lawn playing with the present her dad gave her."

"So what?" Marco asked.

"So . . . " I passed him the photograph. It showed me and Melissa in shorts. And between us a small black-and-white kitten. "So her present was a cat."

Chapter 6

"Look! A kitty door!" Jake pointed.

"Where?" Marco asked.

"See the lines of light? At the bottom of the regular door?"

"Oh, yeah," Marco said. "I wish the moon were out. I can't see a thing."

The four of us were cowering behind a hedge that bordered the Chapmans' lawn. They lived in a pretty normal-looking suburban home. You know: two storeys, a garage, a lawn. Nothing to make you think that the person who lived there was part of a huge alien conspiracy to take over the world.

"Let me just ask you this," Marco whispered. "Why did it have to be Chapman? I was afraid of

45

Chapman even before we found out he was a Controller."

"You're not still upset over that detention he gave you?" I asked. "Look, if you're going to listen to your CD player in maths class with an earphone hidden under your hair, you have to remember not to start singing along."

"Yeah, that was only slightly stupid, Marco," Jake agreed.

"But I still say that Chapman never would have given me a whole week's detention if he was totally human."

"I have a question," Cassie said. "How do we get Melissa's cat to come outside?"

We all looked at her.

"Good question," I admitted.

"I mean, we could hide here in the bushes for a long time. But sooner or later the neighbours are going to notice."

<What does the cat look like?>

Tobias was sitting perched on a nearby tree branch. He was close enough to hear us.

I tried to remember. "Its name is Fluffer, I remember that much. Fluffer McKitty."

"You've got to be kidding." Marco, of course.

I tried to remember back to when I used to hang out with Melissa. "It's black and white. You know, in patches."

<I'll look around. Maybe it's already outside.>

Tobias spread his wings, swooped silently down over our heads, and flapped away into the night.

"You know what we need?" I said. "We need another kitty. We should have thought of that. Then we could have the second cat call out to Fluffer."

Marco turned to stare at me. "Meowfluffer, comeoutmeow, meow come and play meow?"

"Tobias morphed a cat very early on, didn't he?" I asked.

"Yeah," Jake said. "His first morph. The first morph any of us did."

"Rachel, you need to remember if you go in there tonight that you have to stay in cat character," Cassie said. "Most people would just think it was weird if a cat acted strangely. But Chapman may be able to guess what's going on if Fluffer suddenly starts acting un-catlike."

"So you're saying I shouldn't try eating with a fork or changing the channels on the TV?"

Everyone laughed — quietly and nervously, but it was laughter just the same.

Suddenly Tobias dropped out of the sky, then drifted over us in a lazy circle and called down, <Got him.>

He settled back on the branch. He was really

an amazing animal, when you just looked at him as a bird and didn't think about him being a boy trapped in there. I mean, the gaze of a hawk when it is looking right at you is incredibly intimidating. Gentle Tobias now had an expression that looked totally ferocious.

"You're kidding. You found Fluffer?" I asked.

<Hey, it's easy. Spotting prey is what I do. Or what a hawk does, anyway. Actually, there are maybe six or eight cats running around the neighbourhood. Also, three dogs and an amazing amount of rats and mice.>

"Rats?" That got Marco's attention. "Rats? Here? This is suburbia. I mean, it's a lot better than where I live. They have rats?"

<There are rats everywhere,> Tobias said. <Rats and mice and all kinds of plump, juicy . . .> He fell silent, embarrassed.

"Get a grip, Tobias," Marco said. "Don't start eating rats, all right? I don't know if I can have someone who eats rats for a friend."

Sometimes Marco is funny. Sometimes he goes too far. This was one of those times. "Shut up, Marco," I growled.

"I ate a live spider," Jake pointed out. "Does that mean you and I can't be friends?" From his tone of voice I could tell he was angry, too.

None of us knew what Tobias was going through. None of us had ever been in morph for more than two hours. Tobias had been a hawk for more than a week.

Marco realized he'd been a jerk. "Well, yeah, I guess you're right," he muttered. "Besides, I've been known to eat eggplant. So I guess I can't criticize."

That was an apology, or as close as Marco could get to an actual apology.

<The cat we're looking for is just a half block away,> Tobias said. <Follow me.>

He flew off, but kept low. We took off after him. Even flying at minimum speed, Tobias was too fast for us to keep up with, so he had to circle back again and again. We had a hard time keeping him in sight.

"This doesn't look *too* strange," Cassie joked. "The four of us running down the street looking up in the sky."

<There,> Tobias called down. <See that yard with the two trees?>

"Yeah. Just to our left?"

<That's the one. The cat you're looking for is stalking a mouse, right behind the trunk of the nearest tree.>

"OK, we can't all go traipsing over some stranger's yard," I pointed out. "I'll go with Cassie."

Marco held up the kitty carrier we had brought along. "Don't you need this?"

49

"Not yet. I'll grab Fluffer and bring him back over here. You two guys just stand here, looking casual."

Cassie and I stepped on to the lawn. The house was dark. Maybe no one was home. That would be good.

"Go left," I suggested to Cassie. We circled the tree.

"Hey, Fluffer," I said in a high, talking-to-animals voice. "Here, kitty kitty. Remember me?"

"There he is."

"I see him." I squatted down and held my hand out towards the cat. "Hey, Fluffer Fluffer. It's me, Rachel."

Fluffer flattened his ears back along his skull. He looked from me to Cassie and back again.

"Come on, Fluffer, it's me. Come on, boy."

"He's a male? He's a tomcat?" Cassie asked.

"Yeah, I think so."

"Oh, wonderful," Cassie moaned. "Please tell me he's been fixed, at least."

"Have you been fixed, Fluffer McKitty?" I cooed. "Why do we care?" I asked Cassie.

"Because kilogramme for kilogramme, a tomcat is like one of the toughest, most dangerous little things around."

"Who, Fluffer? My little kitty friend Fluffer?"

"Even if he is fixed, a male cat, out at night in

hunting mode?" Cassie shook her head. "We should have worn gloves."

"Oh, come on. He's a sweet kitty cat." To demonstrate just how sweet Fluffer was, I reached a hand for him.

"*Hhhhhhsssssss!*"

In a movement too fast for my human eyes to see, Fluffer swiped out with one paw. Three bloody scratches appeared on the back of my hand and Fluffer shot straight up the tree.

"Owww!" I stuck my injured hand to my mouth.

"Gloves would definitely have been a good idea," Cassie said.

"How are you guys doing?" Jake whispered, just loudly enough for me to hear him.

"Wonderful," I said through gritted teeth. "I'm bleeding and Fluffer is up the tree."

I heard Marco giggle. I expected that. But then I heard Jake giggling, too.

I looked up and saw two glittering yellow-green eyes glaring down from the dark tree.

"This was supposed to be the easy part," I said. "I figured, OK, we go and acquire Fluffer's DNA, and *then* the hard stuff begins."

"We have a cat up a tree," Cassie said dolefully. "You know how hard it is to get a cat down out of a tree?"

"I have a plan," I said. "Tobias, are you up there?"

<Right above you. But I'm *not* going to try and snatch an angry tomcat down out of a tree.>

"That's not what I was going to ask," I said. I took a deep breath. This night was turning weird real fast. "What I need is a mouse."

Chapter 7

<Got something for you. A baby mouse. A *mean* baby mouse. It keeps trying to bite me.> Tobias flew in a low, tight circle overhead, disappearing behind the tree branches, then reappearing. <Are you ready?>

I took a deep breath. I gave him a wave. Sure, I was ready. Why wouldn't I be ready to have a hawk hand me a mouse? Just your normal kind of thing to deal with.

Tobias flew low and slow. I held out my hands, cupped together. With amazing precision and perfect timing, he deposited the mouse in my hands.

"Don't let it bite you!" Cassie warned. "Rabies."

"Wonderful," I muttered. "Just one more fun aspect of this night." Actually, I was glad for the warning. The mouse was squirming in terror, trying to get away. I could feel its tiny little mouse legs scrabbling against my palms.

"You should all get rabies shots," Cassie said. "Seriously. I already have mine. But if we're going to be handling wild animals . . . In the meantime, be careful to keep his teeth away from you."

"I wasn't planning on feeding him my finger," I said.

"Hey, wait." Cassie pried open my hands to get a better look. "That's not a mouse. That's a shrew. See the eyes? They're too small. And the tail is wrong. That's not a baby mouse, Tobias, it's a full-grown shrew."

<Sorry. Is that bad?>

Cassie shrugged. "I don't know. I just know it isn't a mouse."

"Wait a minute," Marco said, beginning to grin. "Rachel is going to become a *shrew*? How will we know when she's changed? How do you *become* what you already are?"

Everyone was too nervous to find the joke very funny. We felt kind of stupid, standing around on some stranger's lawn playing with rodents. I mean, there are times when the whole thing just seems so utterly insane, you know?

"OK, I have to concentrate on acquiring, so everyone shut up," I said.

Acquiring is what we call it when we absorb a sample of the animal's DNA. The DNA is the stuff inside the cells that sort of serves like a how-to manual for making the animal.

When you acquire, you have to think hard about the animal, focusing on it and blocking everything else out. Then the animal kind of goes limp, like it's in a trance. It takes just about a minute.

It was easy to focus on the shrew, what with it squealing in terror and squirming to get out of my hand. But it was gross, definitely gross. I know there's nothing really wrong with shrews, but still. They freak me out a little.

When I was done, I opened my eyes. "OK, little shrew, thanks for your help. You can go now."

"I'm not sure this is a good idea," Jake said doubtfully.

"Really?" Marco was sarcastic. "You're not sure it's a good idea for Rachel to turn into a shrew in order to lure a vicious cat down from a tree so she can morph into that cat and sneak into the assistant principal's house? What worries you about that plan?"

Cassie looked worried, too. "You know, Rachel, usually a cat will play with a mouse a little bit. But sometimes they don't. Sometimes they go right for the neck bite. The mouse — or the shrew — dies instantly."

<Be careful, Rachel,> Tobias said. <I'll be watching, but be careful. I don't want anything to happen to you.>

He "said" it so only I could hear. I could tell, because nobody else reacted.

I looked up at Tobias and winked. I knew he would see it. I rubbed my hands together. "OK, let's do this."

I concentrated once more on the shrew. The shrew was now a part of me. I don't know how it works, but it does. Somehow, thanks to the Andalite technology, the DNA of that shrew was stored away inside me. It was like having a map to guide me as I transformed. Not that I had a clue how I was able to do it.

The first sensation was of shrinking. It's a long, long trip down from being nearly a metre tall to being two centimetres tall. It's like falling. Except that you can feel the ground under your feet the whole time.

One minute I was looking Jake and Marco and Cassie in the face. The next minute their faces seemed to be zooming high up above me. I was falling down the length of their bodies. It was like they were huge skyscrapers and I had jumped off the roof or something.

My outer clothing fell around me like a big,

collapsing circus tent.

It made a slight grinding noise as my back-
bone collapsed into a size smaller than my little
finger. There was the disturbing, not-quite-pain
sensation that goes along with some morphs.
Like you knew it should hurt, but it didn't quite.

I could feel the tail sprout from my tailbone.
A long, hairless tail. Not at all attractive.

My legs practically disappeared, they were so
small. I was a chubby little ball of fur no more
than four centimetres long, with four tiny feet.

Then the fear kicked in. The shrew's fear.

It hit me so hard I began to shake. I rattled
with terror. I quaked with terror.

I was surrounded! Predators everywhere! I
could smell them. I could see them — huge,
looming, slow-moving creatures standing over
me.

"Rachel? You OK down there?" It was Cassie.
She lifted the folds of my clothing off of me.

I heard the voice and sort of understood it,
but it was more like distant thunder. It didn't really mean anything. At least not to the shrew.

It was looking for a way out. Its brain might
have been terrified, but it was also amazingly
smart. It was evaluating every possible escape
route. It was measuring the distance between the
three sets of legs. One set of legs moved slightly.

I was off like a shot.

57

Running! Running! Blades of grass seemed two metres tall. Twigs were like fallen trees that I had to scramble over. My little feet moved with incredible speed. I scooted past a beetle that seemed to me to be as big as a dog.

"Rachel, you have to get control!"

I knew they were right. I even sort of understood what they meant. But the terror was so strong. The urge to survive was so powerful.

And at the same time there were other feelings. Hunger. I smelled nuts. I smelled dead flesh. I even smelled the maggots squirming on the dead flesh.

And I wanted them. I know it's too gross, but I wanted to eat those maggots.

Heavy pounding footsteps behind me! I turned sharply and ducked under a bush. The steps went barrelling by before stopping and turning back towards me.

They were faster than I was, but not as agile. I could get away. I could get away and find that dead smell and gorge!

<Rachel, it's Tobias. The shrew is in control. You have to assert yourself! Tell it to stop running.>

Fear! Hunger!

<Rachel, listen to me. You're getting away from us. You have to take charge.>

Fear! Hunger! Run!

58

Grass and twigs and dirt. Low scratchy branches over my head. The smell of food. The smell of a dog that had urinated on this bush.

More loud footsteps and far-off rumbling voices yelling. They were trying to catch me. But I was fast! I was clever!

But not clever enough. I ran out from under the bush.

Like a shadow inside of a shadow, I felt it descend on me. Terror like nothing I'd felt before swept over me. Something deep, deep inside my shrew brain cried out.

It was the ultimate fear! The ultimate horror! It was the enemy I could not defeat!

And it was coming for me!

Chapter 8

I dodged, but too slowly. Huge talons closed around me and suddenly my little feet were running in air.

<OK, Rachel. It's OK. It's just me. I have you.>

The voice was in my head. I understood the words. It cut through the terror at last. I held on to that voice.

<Relax, Rachel.>

I looked down and with my dim shrew eyesight saw the shadows shooting past down below.

<I have you, Rachel. Try to be calm. Think about something human. Think about school. Remember school?>

School? Yes. I remembered school.

Quite suddenly the shrew mind lost the battle for control. It was like a switch had been flipped. I was in charge. I knew what I was. I knew *who* I was.

<I'm OK, Tobias,> I said. <You can set me down.>

He circled around and landed with perfect gentleness on the ground.

<Did my talons hurt you?>

<No. I don't think so. I'm fine.>

"You OK, Rachel?" Jake's voice.

<Yes. Boy, that was totally different than the elephant brain. Or the eagle. They're both so calm and mellow compared to this mind.>

"It's like Jake's lizard," Cassie suggested. "He had a panic reaction, too. The other animals we morphed were all kind of big, dominant animals — gorilla, tiger. My horse was skittish, though."

<Look, let's just do this and get it over with, OK?> I said. <I'm not enjoying the shrew experience.> That was the understatement of all time. I could still smell death and hear the thousands of feasting maggots. And to me those things still meant dinner. I was horribly hungry.

"Are you really sure you're going to be able to maintain down there?" Marco asked. I saw him peering down at me from a million miles up. "You still look a little nervous. Your tail is twitching and your little nose is sniffing like crazy."

<Yeah, I know. I'm still nervous. Let's just do this. You'll have to take me back to the tree where Fluffer is. I don't know what direction it is.>

Before I could object, Marco reached down and scooped me into his hands. He held me up and looked into my eyes. "I've never seen you look lovelier, Rachel. Very cover girl."

We walked down the block. Marco set me down at the bottom of the tree where Fluffer was still hiding out on a high branch.

<You guys had better back off a little,> I said.

"Not *too* far," Jake said. "We have to be able to get between you and Fluffer fast."

<Oh, I can kick Fluffer's butt,> I said, joking. I guess I felt a little embarrassed about having let the shrew take control of me.

"Uh-huh," Marco said dryly. "Cat versus mouse. Who would you bet on?"

"Haven't you ever seen *Tom and Jerry?*" Cassie asked. "Mouse, definitely. Besides, she's not a mouse."

Let me tell you something: it is no fun sitting around in a shrew's tiny body, waiting to see whether a huge cat is going to decide to climb down and kill you. It is one of the least fun things that I've ever done. I had the shrew brain under control, but that didn't change the fact that the shrew was about as scared as a shrew can be. Between being snatched up by a hawk and now waiting to see if the shrew's other deadly enemy was going to attack . . . I mean, the shrew was definitely in a state of panic.

She was not a happy shrew.

I was so preoccupied thinking about the shrew's hunger that I missed what happened next. I didn't even notice until I heard the sound of scraping tree bark just a centimetre over my head. Fluffer was dropping through the air right on top of me!

I froze!

Jake and Marco did not freeze.

Marco grabbed Fluffer in mid-pounce. Fluffer rewarded him with a nasty slash of his claws. Marco yelled and almost dropped the cat. Jake grabbed Fluffer by the nape of the neck and Cassie ran up with the animal carrier.

The three of them managed to stuff the squalling, hissing, slashing Fluffer into the carrier and close the door.

I was already morphing out of the shrew body as fast as I could.

"I'm bleeding!" Marco cried.

"We're all bleeding," Cassie said matter-of-factly. "I told you guys: Kitties can be nasty when you get on their nerves."

I was shooting up from the ground, regaining my normal body.

"Ugh! Ugh! I'm never doing that morph again," I said, as soon as I had a normal tongue and lips. I looked over my shoulder to make sure I didn't still have that creepy tail. Nothing. I was me again. I was in my morphing outfit and with no shoes on, but I was human again.

I shuddered. The memory of the shrew's brain and its fear and hunger made my flesh creep. I was fighting a powerful urge to throw up. I felt sick in a way that is mostly in your head.

Jake looked at me and shook his head. "I should have done it. I should have used my lizard morph to lure the cat down from the tree."

I shook my head. "No. That freaked you out."

"And now you're the one who's freaked out," Jake said. "But don't worry, you'll get over it. Mostly. At least *you* didn't eat a spider."

"Yeah. Look, I'm just tired, OK? Let me acquire this pain-in-the-butt cat and get on with this."

"Are you still up for it?" Cassie asked. "Acquiring two new morphs in one night?"

"I shouldn't have let you do the mouse. Shrew. Whatever," Jake said. He was still looking guilty.

"Look, it was my idea, right? Besides, since when do you *let* me do things? What are you, my master? I don't think so. Come on." I squared my shoulders and put on a brave smile. "Let me see how Fluffer likes me, now that I'm bigger than he is."

I guess Fluffer was tired of causing trouble. He was actually asleep in the cat carrier. Sleeping like nothing at all was going on. A typical cat. He even purred as I acquired him.

When I was done, I noticed Cassie smiling at me.

"What?" I asked her.

"I was just thinking how you look like the same old Rachel, but now you also have an elephant, a shrew, an eagle, and a cat inside you. That's four morphs. That's more than any of us." She looked thoughtful. "We don't really know very much about this morphing thing still. I wonder if there is a limit to how many morphs you can do."

"I guess we'll find out," Marco said darkly. "Probably at the worst possible time."

I wondered if they were right. It was definitely a strange, powerful feeling, knowing that I could become four very different animals. Strange and powerful and disturbing. Inside of me I had animals that ate each other. It wasn't a good image.

Suddenly I felt exhausted. "Look, guys . . . I've acquired Fluffer now. But maybe we should do the rest of this tomorrow night. I'm . . . I don't know if I'm at my best right now."

"Another night," Jake agreed. He looked relieved. I think he was worried about me. That's the way Jake is.

"I guess we can let Fluffer go now," Cassie said. She opened the carrier and the cat climbed out cautiously.

I watched him run off into the night.

"Probably going off to kill your shrew," Marco speculated.

The idea made me shudder all over again.

Chapter 9

"**A**aaaaaaaahhh! Aaaaah! Aaaaaaaaaah!"

"Wake up. Rachel, wake up!"

"*Aaah!* Oh. Oh. Oh." I sat up. I was gasping for air. It was dark, but I could just make out Jordan's face. She was shaking me awake.

I felt my face. Lips. Eyes. Nose.

I patted myself down frantically. Human. I was human. No fur. No tail. Human.

The details of the dream came rushing up to my consciousness.

"Oh, no," I moaned. I threw back the covers and stumbled to my feet. I staggered towards the bathroom door. The bathroom connects my room and the room Jordan and Sara share. I tried to turn on the light but missed the switch. I dropped

67

to my knees in front of the toilet and threw up.

Jordan kept saying, "Are you all right, Rachel? Are you all right? I'd better get Mum."

"No," I said, as soon as I could talk. "No, I'm fine. Don't wake Mum up." Fortunately, little Sara can sleep through anything.

I brushed my teeth and drank some water. I looked sheepishly at Jordan. She looks nothing like me. I guess I look more like my dad, and Jordan is like this smaller version of my mum, dark hair and dark eyes. She looked pretty scared.

"I'm OK," I said again. "Just a bad dream. I guess it made me kind of sick, is all. But I'm fine now."

Jordan relaxed a little. "Must have been *some* dream."

"I guess so. I can't even remember it now. You know how it is. Dreams fade away so you can't even remember them."

"I can't believe you would just forget a dream that made you scream *and* hurl."

I shrugged. "I've never been very good at re-membering dreams. You better get back to bed."

She looked at me solemnly. "I know I'm just your little sister by two years, but you would tell me if something bad was happening to you, right? I mean, I wouldn't tell Mum or anyone. You could trust me."

I smiled and drew her into a hug. "I know I

can trust you. If anything bad was going on, I'd tell you." It was a lie, of course, and the lie made me feel even worse. I trusted Jordan. I knew in my heart that she was not a Controller.

Of course, that's just what Jake had said about Tom.

I hugged my sister a little closer. I hated the way suspicion had crept into every part of my mind. I hated the way I wasn't sure, not really, totally sure, that I could trust her.

"Good night," I said. "Thanks for rescuing me from that nightmare. Whatever it was."

She started to walk away. Then she turned, lit from behind by the garish bathroom light. "Before you started screaming, you were yelling something."

"What?" I asked, afraid of the answer.

She looked puzzled. "I think it was 'maggots.' Something like that."

I forced a shaky smile. "Good night, Jordan."

I crawled back into my bed. The pillow was soaked with sweat. The sheets were clammy.

Maggots. Squirming, crawling, busy little white maggots. They were all over a piece of rotting meat and fur. In my dream it was a dead cat. A dead cat covered with vermin eating the decayed flesh.

A shrew was getting in on the feast, eating at the dead flesh and the living maggots with equal enjoyment.

In my dream I knew: I *was* that shrew.

"You look tired," Jake said the next morning. We took the same bus to school.

"Thanks," I said grumpily.

"Didn't get enough sleep last night?"

"I guess not, if I look as bad as you say."

"I didn't say you looked bad, I just said you looked tired." He hesitated. He glanced over his shoulder, checking to see whether anyone was listening. Fortunately, the noise level was pretty high in the bus. Jake lowered his voice and leaned close to my ear. "You didn't get creeped out by the shrew, did you?"

"Why? Just because I'm a girl, you think the shrew bothered me more than it would have bothered you or Marco?"

"No, that's not it at all," he said earnestly. "It's just . . . see, when I did the lizard morph, that bothered me. I had nightmares — "

"Nightmares?" I said it too loudly. Then I lowered my voice back to a whisper. "Nightmares?"

"Oh, yeah. Definitely. When I morphed the tiger I had dreams, too, but not nightmares."

"What kind of dreams?"

He smiled. "Kind of cool, really. Stalking through a dark forest at night. I was hunting something. It was like I wanted to catch it, but at

70

the same time it was like if I didn't catch it that would be OK, too. Because just running and creeping and then running some more through the woods was the best thing in the world."

I nodded. "I felt like that after the elephant morph. It was this incredible feeling of being huge and invincible. Like I could never even possibly be afraid of anything."

"But the shrew was different, wasn't it? Same with the lizard."

"I guess it's the different characters of the animals. Maybe some are good matches for our human brains. Maybe others aren't." I looked out the window for a while. Then I said, "You know what scares me?"

To my surprise, Jake nodded. "Yeah. You're afraid that someday we might have to morph into bugs."

I shuddered. "I don't think I'll be willing to do that. I think that may be too much."

"Well, your next assignment is a cat. Tobias was a cat. He said it was amazingly cool. He liked it. Just like I really enjoy being a dog. Sometimes when I'm feeling depressed, I really wish I could just morph. Dogs know how to have fun."

The bus pulled up in front of the school. "Another day of school. Normal life." I looked over the crowd of kids milling around on the lawn and on the steps. I spotted Melissa.

"See you later, Jake," I said. "Thanks."

"No problem. We're all in this together."

I made my way down the bus aisle and ran to catch up to Melissa. But when I got close I saw that her eyes were red and swollen. She'd been crying.

I didn't know what to do. In the old days I would have just run right up to her and asked what was the matter.

"Hey, Melissa, how's it going?"

She looked at me, confused. "What?"

"I said, how's it going?"

She shook her head slowly, like she couldn't believe I was even talking to her. "What do you care?"

"Melissa. Of course I care. What's wrong?"

Her eyes went kind of blank. She seemed to be looking at nothing but the air right in front of her face. "What's wrong? Everything is wrong. And nothing is wrong. But just the same, everything is wrong."

"Melissa, what are you talking about?"

"Forget it," she said. She started to walk away.

I grabbed her arm. "Look, you can talk to me. I'm still your friend. Nothing has changed."

"Leave me alone," she said grimly. "Everything has changed. Every*one* has changed. You stopped being my friend. And my mum and dad . . . "

"What?" I pressed her.

The bell rang loud and shrill.

"I have to go." She pulled her arm away.

What could I do? I let her go. I wondered what she had started to say about her father. Had she discovered what her father was? What her father had become?

I walked up the steps of the school with my head lowered in thought. As I opened the school door, I ran right into someone.

"Hey, hey, watch where you're going, young lady."

"Mr Chapman!" I recoiled in fear.

See, you have to realize that this was the man who had once directed a Hork-Bajir soldier to kill us all if he caught us. Kill us and only save our heads for identification.

That kind of thing sticks in your mind.

He peered at me. "What's the matter with you, Rachel? A little jumpy this morning?"

I nodded. "Yes, sir. I guess I didn't sleep too well."

"Bad dreams?" he asked.

My mouth was dry. "I guess so, Mr Chapman."

He smiled. A normal, human smile. His eyes even crinkled up a little as he grinned down at me. "Well, shake it off. Nightmares aren't real, you know."

"At least not most of the time," I said to myself.

Chapter 10

We couldn't go to the Chapmans' the next night because Marco and I both had papers we had to write. And the night after that was Cassie's dad's birthday.

But finally, there we were again on the street outside the Chapmans' house. It was a little before eight.

Fluffer was out of the house, smelling a fence post four blocks over, where another cat had left his scent. At least, that's what Tobias reported.

"Are you ready?" Jake asked me.

I nodded.

"Are you sure?" Cassie asked. "You can put this off if you want. We don't have to do this tonight."

"The sooner the better," I said. "We all know something is wrong in that house. Melissa is still my friend. Maybe somehow I can help her."

"Your job is not to help Melissa Chapman," Marco pointed out. "You're supposed to be spying on Chapman. You're supposed to be finding some way for us to get at the Yeerks, so that we can all turn into wild animals and get ourselves killed."

"I know why I'm doing this, Marco," I said.

He nodded. "OK. Well, take care of yourself in there. That's an assistant principal you're dealing with. He finds out you've turned into a cat and gone sneaking around his house, that will be after-school detention for like a year."

We all laughed. As if detention were the thing I had to fear. Marco can be obnoxious, but on the other hand, he can make you laugh right when you really need to.

"I'm ready," I said. I waved my arms at the dark sky above. Tobias swooped down, opened his wings to slow his speed, and settled on the fence beside us.

"How does it look up there, Tobias?" Jake asked.

<Looks fine. The cat is nowhere near the house. There's no one out walking around, except way over on Loughlin Street. There are a couple of cars, but not coming towards you.>

"You know, you could have quite a future in

76

burglary," Marco said to Tobias. "You and I can burglarize places, and Jake can be Spiderman and catch us."

"OK, I'm ready to do this," I announced. "As ready as I'm going to get, anyway."

Tobias sent me a private message. <Rachel, if you get into any trouble, just try and make it outside. I can lift you out of any danger.>

I prepared to morph. I concentrated on Fluffer. It was easy to do. I had a very clear mental image of Fluffer dropping down out of that tree, ready to kill me when I was a shrew.

Inside my own body, Fluffer's DNA was stored, ready to be used. All I had to do was concentrate . . . concentrate. . . .

Each morphing is different. Especially the first time, when you can't even think about controlling how it happens. Even Cassie can't control the first morph.

In the case of Fluffer, it started with fur. Black fur came first, and then the white fur began to grow. The fur had almost completely grown in while I was still mostly human. I had luxurious fur on my arms. On my legs. On my face. Fur and whiskers, with everything else pretty much the same.

"Oh, that is cool!" Cassie said. She was staring at me and grinning this huge grin. "That is way cool. You look great."

77

Marco and Jake nodded agreement.

"It's kind of weird, but also kind of pretty," Marco said. "I'm thinking you could do commercials for cat food. You sing a little song, maybe dance a little. Forget Morris the cat. You would rule."

I began to shrink. But it was strange, because as I shrank and my outer clothing slithered off me, I didn't feel like I was getting smaller. I felt more like I was getting stronger.

It was like I was shedding all this unnecessary stuff, these clumsy long legs, these ridiculous weak arms. I felt like I'd been boiled down to my absolute essentials. Like I wasn't even made out of plain old flesh and bones any more.

I felt like liquid steel.

I didn't feel the fear of the shrew. I didn't feel the total confidence of the elephant, either, or of the eagle.

This was different. There was fear, sure. But underneath the fear was confidence. The cat knew there were enemies out there, but he also knew he could handle it.

I felt . . . tough. That was it — tough.

Then the cat's senses started sending messages to my brain.

<Whoa!> I yelled in surprise. <Suddenly it isn't nighttime any more! I mean, wow. Talk about night vision!>

"A cat's vision at night is about eight times stronger than a human's," Cassie said helpfully. "I looked it up."

"*Eight* times?" Marco repeated. "Not seven, or nine? How do they measure that?"

But it wasn't just how *well* I saw that was strange. It was *what* I noticed.

A human being will notice colours, for example. Now, a cat can see colours, more or less. He just isn't interested in colours. It's like, OK, that thing is red. Who cares?

What cats really notice is movement. If anything moves, even the tiniest bit, the cat sees it. I was standing there on the grass, looking around with my big cat eyes, and I saw nothing but movement.

I saw every blade of grass that moved in the breeze. I saw every bug that crawled across those blades of grass. I saw every bird in every tree as it fluffed its wings. And boy, did I see the mice and the squirrels and the rats.

There was a mouse no more than six metres away. I could see the individual whiskers on his little snout when they twitched.

Things that were not moving were boring to me. If the mouse just stayed completely still, I would forget he was even there.

"How are you doing?" Jake asked me.

I had no trouble at all hearing his voice. But it

was irrelevant. It had no meaning. The mouse was making a tiny little scritching sound as it worked its little teeth around a nut, trying to chew it open.

I cared about that sound. I cared about that sound a lot.

"Rachel, can you hear us? It's me, Cassie."

<Yes, I can hear you. I just can't seem to concentrate very well on you. There are so many other things to hear and see and smell.>

"Well, at least she's not running around out of control," Marco said.

Suddenly I sensed something over my head, a shape, a shadow, a figure. Lightning quick, I turned my head. My ears flattened back against my skull. The hair on my back stood up and my tail puffed out to three times its normal size. My claws extended. I drew back my mouth and showed my teeth.

It all happened in a split second. I was ready for battle.

And whatever this was attacking me, I wanted it to know it would be sorry it messed with Fluffer McKitty.

"*Hhhhhiisssss!*"

Chapter 11

I was ready to fight. I was *pumped.* Kill or be killed.

It is so cool when you feel the razor-sharp claws sliding out of your delicate-looking pink pads.

"Rachel, take a pill, girl, it's just Tobias," Cassie said soothingly. "Tobias? I think maybe you'd better stay away," she called up to the sky. "Cats are genetically programmed to be afraid of large birds."

She was right. The shadow of Tobias scared me pretty good. It was strange, because it was a fear I shared with the shrew.

But it was a different type of fear than the shrew's. This was more like I was angry, too. Only

81

that wasn't quite it, either. I guess it wasn't a real emotion at all. Basically, when I'd hissed I was just trying to communicate. And the message I was trying to communicate was, "Don't mess with me. You may be bigger than me, you may scare me, you may make me run away, but if I have to I am ready to fight."

That was my whole cat message to the world: Don't mess with me. Don't get in my way, don't try to touch me if I don't want to be touched, don't try to keep me from getting what I want.

I was self-contained. I was complete. I didn't need anything but myself. It seemed lonely to my human self, but at the same time, it was all very calm somehow.

<I'm OK,> I said. <I think I'm pretty much in control.>

"What's it like?" Cassie asked.

<It's like . . . You know those old cowboy movies with Clint Eastwood? He's a gunslinger and he walks into the saloon and everyone kind of gets out of his way? And how he's not really looking for trouble, but you'd better not make him mad? That's what it's like. It's like I'm Clint Eastwood.>

"Can you do this, do you think?" Jake asked me.

<Oh, yeah. I can do *anything*.>

"Don't let the cat's arrogance get you into

trouble," Marco advised. "Keep a little of your good old human fear." He paused. "Oh, I forgot, mighty Rachel doesn't have any good old human fear. So here's what you do: Borrow some of *my* good old human fear. I have plenty to spare."

"He's right, Rachel," Cassie agreed. "Keep focused. Between your own natural attitude and the cat's 'tude, you could get cocky."

I cast a glance back towards the mouse. He had broken into the nut at last. I could kill him. I was sure of that. He was a plump little mouse, and I would catch him easily. But I wasn't hungry. So he'd get to live a while longer.

<No problem,> I said.

"We'll be here if you get into a mess," Cassie reassured me.

<I'll meow if I need help. Don't worry. I'm in control now. It'll be fine.>

But the truth is, I was lying, just a little. See, I wasn't completely in control of the cat. For some reason I didn't *want* to completely control the cat. I kind of liked his arrogance. It made me feel more sure of myself. And despite what the others thought about me, I needed all the confidence I could get.

"The morph clock is ticking," Cassie said. "It's quarter to eight. Remember that."

I headed at an easy trot down the road towards the Chapman home. As soon as I started moving I thought, *Oh, man, if I could just keep some of this for my next gymnastics class.*

It was like grace beyond any grace you can imagine as a human. I passed a wooden fence. There was a railing up high, maybe a metre up. I looked up at it and then, before I could even think about it, I leaped. My powerful hind legs coiled up and released.

I sailed through the air. One metre straight up, and I was an animal that stood only about thirty centimetres tall. It was the same as a human being just leaping to the top of a two-storey building.

And it was totally *nothing*. It was just automatic. I wanted to jump, so I did. I wanted to stick the landing on a narrow four-centimetre-wide rail, and of course, no problem.

Compared to a cat, the best gymnast who ever lived is like a big staggering cow or something.

"Um, Rachel, what exactly are you doing?" Jake asked.

They were all standing there looking at me. I had totally forgotten they were still around.

<Just practising,> I said. I jumped back down to the grass. OK, get the job done first, I ordered myself sternly. You can worry about the Kitty Olympics later.

I started once more towards the house, but this time something forced me to stop. It was a telephone pole. The smell that emanated from it was overpowering. I went over to it. I sniffed it again and again in short snorts of air. The air was trapped in a series of chambers above my palette. It would be held there even while I went on breathing. That way I could get every possible bit of information from that smell.

It was definitely a tom's scent. A tomcat had marked this pole by peeing on it. He was a dominant cat. Very dominant. His smell made me nervous. Not afraid, just a little less arrogant than I had been. If this cat appeared, I would have to submit. I would have to make myself smaller and less threatening and accept his dominance.

Or I could fight him and get my butt kicked.

It was just the way things were. It was all there in the smell of his urine, where any cat could read it.

I resumed trotting towards the Chapman home.

<Rachel, are you sure you're in control?> Tobias's voice was in my head. <Why did you stop to sniff that pole?>

<I figured I should look like a real cat,> I said. <I was just playing the part.>

<If you say so,> he said doubtfully. <Just remember: It's fun being an animal for a while. Not so fun when it's permanent. The two-hour clock is ticking. Tick tock.>

85

That got my attention. It was like a dash of cold water in my face. I focused my human mind and took greater control over the cat's mind. But it wasn't easy. The cat's mind did not even understand the notion of obeying.

So I used something the cat would respond to. I conjured up the memory of the big tom's smell. That triggered the cat's submissiveness. I felt my part of the collective mind grow larger.

<You're almost there,> Tobias said. <This is the right yard.>

<Yes, I know. My scent is everywhere. This whole area smells of me. This is home. This is all mine.>

<Rachel, this is all *Chapman's*. And Chapman belongs to Visser Three. Don't forget that.>

I trotted to the cat door. Chapman. Visser Three. Big deal. I was a combination of Rachel and Fluffer. What did I care about Chapman and Visser Three?

The light inside the house was bright. My eyes adjusted instantly. My nose picked up the smell of cat food, too dry and old to interest me. I also smelled the humans: Melissa, Mr Chapman, and Ms Chapman. Don't ask me how I knew that what I smelled were those three people. I just knew.

I spotted a cockroach in the dust balls in the dark beneath the refrigerator. No interest to me.

Roaches made interesting scritchy noises sometimes, and they were fun to watch run. But they smelled wrong. They were not prey.

Swift movements!

Feet. Human feet. I didn't bother looking up. It was Ms Chapman.

High-pitched sounds coming from the motor of the refrigerator. They were annoying. There were also the sounds of birds outside. They had a nest up under the eaves.

Then the sound of Melissa's voice.

Where was she? I didn't see her anywhere. The sound was muffled.

I tried to focus. My ears moved to point towards the sound. It came from above me. Above and far away.

She was in her bedroom, that's where. I couldn't hear the words clearly, but I knew that she was muttering to herself.

I trotted across the kitchen floor. I knew — as *Rachel* — I knew I *should* be afraid. But I couldn't be afraid. Everything here smelled like me. My scent glands had left their marks all over — on that door, on that cupboard, on that chair. It reassured me.

The big dominant tomcat's smell was not in here. No, there were no other cats in here at all. Only human smells, and to me those were not very important.

I left the kitchen and paused at the corner between the hallway and the family room. Chapman was there, in the living room. I could smell him. He was just sitting on the couch. I glanced at him and walked on.

But then I stopped. My human brain sensed something wrong with the picture. Chapman was just sitting on the couch. No TV. No music. He wasn't reading a book or a newspaper. Just sitting.

I turned back to the kitchen. I looked up at Ms Chapman. She was doing something at the sink. Maybe washing dishes. No, she was cutting vegetables. But again, no TV. No music. She wasn't humming to herself. She wasn't talking to herself the way my mum does when she's working in the kitchen.

Not right. Something was not right with either of the Chapmans.

I went back to the hallway. There were stairs leading up to the bedrooms. From the hallway I could hear Melissa more clearly. I concentrated, trying to ignore the fascinating sounds of the birds under the eaves. I focused on the human sounds of Melissa's voice.

". . . divided by the square root . . . no, wait. No, square root times . . . Is that right?"

She was doing her homework. Her maths homework, obviously.

Like I *should* be doing, I thought. I had a pang of guilt. Instead of doing my homework, I was creeping around my friend's house spying on her and her parents.

I tried to find a clock. I had to watch the time. At nine forty-five my two hours would be up. I wanted to be out of morph and back in my normal body long before then. Hopefully, I could still get home and do my maths homework and at least do some of the reading for social studies class.

I spotted a clock. It was over the mantel, between pictures of the Chapmans and Melissa. The clock said three minutes to eight. I had plenty of time.

Sudden movement!

Oh, just Chapman standing up.

The cat part of me wasn't interested in Chapman one way or the other. But I forced myself to pay attention. It was important to watch him. That was why I was here.

Is he prey? The cat brain seemed to be asking.

Yes. Yes, I told the cat brain.

Chapman is our prey.

89

Chapter 12

I followed Chapman as he headed down the hallway. Either he didn't notice me, or else he didn't care.

He opened a door that let loose a flood of smells. Dampness. Mildew. Bugs.

<Rachel? How are you doing in there?>

I jerked in surprise. A very un-catlike movement.

It was Tobias. He had to be fairly close for me to be able to hear his thought-speech. He must be on the roof or perched on a nearby tree branch. I strained my sensitive cat hearing. The birds under the eaves were silent. They were afraid of the big hawk.

<I'm fine,> I said. <But you scared me half to death!>

<Sorry. I was just worried.>

<Well, don't worry. I'm following Chapman down to the basement.>

<Why?>

<Because that's where he's going. Duh,> I said. Somehow, Tobias's human words were annoying me. He wanted me to pay attention to him and it was hard to do. The cat didn't care about his words. The cat just wanted to go down and look around the basement. Fortunately, that's what I wanted to do, too.

I trotted down the rough wooden stairs after Chapman. Very weird, by the way. Going downstairs as a cat gave me a feeling of vertigo. I mean, I was going down head first. It's strange.

<Look, Tobias, I appreciate you looking out for me. But I'm kind of busy right now.>

<I understand. I can't hear you very well, anyway. You're getting farther away.>

<Yeah, I'm going down.> I waited. He said nothing. <Tobias?> I called. But there was no answer. We're still learning about thought-speech. We know there are limits on how far it can be "heard." But we aren't sure what the limits are.

The basement had panelling all around. The ceiling was bare wood and full of spiders and other interesting things. No mice, though. Nothing that could be considered actual prey. But many things that might be fun to chase.

Chapman is the prey, I reminded myself. *We are hunting Chapman.*

There was a sort of TV room with a pool table and some old chairs and a couch. But it was obvious that no one had used them for a long time. There were no human scents on them. There was dust everywhere and I could hear that there were spiders inside the TV set.

The only part of the basement that appeared to have been used was a path right across the floor. I smelled the scents that Chapman had tracked there with his shoes.

He walked in a straight line across the basement to a door. It was a simple white-painted door. Chapman pulled a set of keys out of his pocket. He unlocked the white door.

He opened it and stepped through. Nearly two metres beyond the white door was a second door. This one was made of gleaming steel. It looked like the door to a bank vault.

Beside the steel door, there was a small, square white panel of light. Chapman pressed his hand against it.

The steel door opened. It slid into the wall like the doors on *Star Trek.*

I knew I had to go after him. But my human

mind was afraid. And my cat mind didn't see any reason why I should walk into that dark place. To both of us, it felt like a trap. Like a place we couldn't get out of.

But I *had* to. I had to go in there. That was the whole point of this spying trip.

And Chapman was my prey.

At the last second, just as the door swooshed shut, I bounded into the room.

It was dark at first, not that it bothered me. Then Chapman turned on a low light. It was strange, because I could actually see better in the dark than I could with the low light.

There was a sort of desk set into the wall. It was grey steel and very unusual-looking. There were more little light panels in various cheerful colours. And there was something that looked like a small but complicated spotlight hanging down from the ceiling. In front of the desk was a chair. A totally normal office-type chair. Chapman sat in it.

He ran his hands over a blue panel. Then he looked at his watch. He sat patiently, waiting.

For about a minute, nothing happened. I tried to look nonchalant, like I had just happened to wander in. But at the same time I was careful to stay behind Chapman so he wouldn't see me.

I remembered Jake's warning. About how anyone else would just assume I was a plain old cat.

But Chapman knew about morphing. The Yeerks knew about the Andalite morphing technology. So if Chapman or any Controller ever saw an animal acting the wrong way, they could suspect the truth.

Suddenly a brilliant light snapped on.

My cat eyes adjusted instantly, but even so, the light was painfully bright. It came from the little spotlight thing. Chapman turned around in his chair to face the light.

The light began to change. It took shape. It turned different colours.

The four hooves appeared. The bluish fur. The many-fingered hands. The flat, intelligent face with no mouth and only slits for a nose. The penetrating, almond-shaped main eyes.

Then the strange extra eyes, mounted on stalks that turned this way and that, looking around the room. Last came the tail, the wicked, curved, scorpionlike tail.

An Andalite. Just like the Andalite prince who had given us our powers.

But I knew this was no true Andalite. Dread washed over me. Dread too strong for even my cat brain to ignore.

This was no true Andalite. This was the only Andalite body ever seized and taken over by the Yeerks. The only Andalite-Controller in all the galaxy.

This was Visser Three. Leader of the Yeerk invasion force. The evil creature who could morph into monsters acquired from all over the universe.

This was Visser Three, the creature who had murdered the Andalite prince while we cowered in terror.

This was Visser Three, who had nearly killed us all in the hell of the Yeerk pool.

"Welcome, Visser," Chapman said in a very humble voice. "Iniss two two six of the Sulp Niaar pool submits to you. May the Kandrona shine and strengthen you."

"And you, Iniss two two six," Visser Three said.

I was shocked to hear the Visser's voice. In his Andalite body he had no mouth. Andalites communicate telepathically, just the way I do when I'm in a morph.

The second shock came from what they had said to each other. "Iniss two two six." That had to be the name of the Yeerk slug who controlled Chapman.

The cat part of my brain was busy with a different question. Was this apparition real? No. There was no scent. No scent at all. Only light and shadows.

It was only a hologram, I knew. But it was a very convincing hologram. Visser Three seemed almost solid. He looked around as though he could see from his holographic eyes.

I prayed he wouldn't look at me.

"Report, Iniss."

"Yes, Visser."

Part of me just wanted to run. Even a hologram of Visser Three makes your skin crawl. But now that he had figured out it wasn't real, the cat part of me was just bored.

I realized why I could hear Visser Three — the hologram projector must not be able to transmit thought-speech. It translated it into regular speech.

"Is there progress on locating the Andalite bandits?"

"No, Visser. Nothing yet."

I knew who he meant by "Andalite bandits." That was us, the Animorphs.

"I want them found. I want them found NOW!"

Chapman jumped back in surprise at the Visser's command. I could smell fear on him.

In a calmer tone, Visser Three went on. "This cannot go on, Iniss two two six, it cannot go on. The Council of Thirteen will hear of it. They will wonder why I reported to them that all Andalite ships near this planet had been destroyed and all the Andalites killed. They will be suspicious.

They will be angry. And when the Council of Thirteen is angry with me, I am angry with you."

Chapman was literally quivering. I smelled human sweat. And I smelled something else. Something not totally human. It was very faint . . . was that the Yeerk itself I was smelling? Was I smelling the Yeerk slug in Chapman's head?

It seemed impossible. But there was some strange smell. Something . . . something . . . I concentrated all my cat mind on analysing the smell.

"What is *that*?"

Chapman swivelled in his chair.

I looked up and froze. Chapman was staring right at me. And worse, much worse, Visser Three's stalk eyes were focused on me, too.

"It's called a cat," Chapman said nervously. "An Earth species used as a pet. The humans keep them close and find comfort in them."

"Why is it in here?"

"It belongs to the girl. My . . . the host's daughter."

"I see," Visser Three said. "Well, kill it. Kill it immediately."

Chapter 13

*K*ill it. Kill it immediately.

I wanted to run. I wanted to panic.

But some strange combination of the cat's cunning and my own intelligence came together and saved me.

I didn't so much as flick a whisker. If I had, I would have been dead. I knew that for a fact. If I'd reacted like I'd understood, they would have known for sure that I was no normal cat.

Visser Three's hologram watched me closely. All four of his Andalite eyes were focused on me now. And behind that gentle Andalite expression, I could feel the razor-sharp focus of the powerful, evil Yeerk.

Chapman, too, was staring at me. He had the same look in his eyes that he had when he caught someone trying to skip out of school.

I was terrified. Or at least the Rachel part of me was terrified. Fluffer couldn't have cared less. He sensed my concern, but he had none of his own. There were no birds of prey here. There were no dogs. There were no smells of dominant cats. There was only a sort of three-dimensional picture that had no scent. And Chapman. Chapman might be prey, or he might not, but he was certainly no threat.

"It could be an Andalite," Visser Three said. "Destroy it."

In response I said, "Meow."

Visser Three glared at me. "What is that?"

"It's . . . it's . . . the s-s-sound a cat makes, Visser. I b-b-believe it wishes to eat."

SAWWWAPP!

Suddenly, without warning, Visser Three whipped his tail at me. A dangerous, half-metre, scythe-shaped blade arced towards me at a speed no human could hope to evade.

But I wasn't just a human.

In a tenth of the time it took to blink, I had seen the sudden motion and I was crouched down, ears back, teeth bared. My paw, claws outstretched, swiped at the tail blade.

My paw went straight through the hologram. And the blade, nothing but a projection, swept through me.

"Ha, ha, ha."

It took me a second to make sense of the sound. It was Visser Three laughing.

Chapman seemed amazed, too. Like he had never heard the Visser laugh. Like it wasn't even possible to imagine the Visser laughing.

"What a ferocious little beast," Visser Three said approvingly. "See how he did not back away or run? I am many times his size and yet he struck at me. A pity that the species is too small to serve as a host."

"Yes, a pity," Chapman said warily.

"Kill it," Visser Three said. "What better form for an Andalite to use? Better kill it, just to be safe."

"Yes, Visser," Chapman said. "O-o-only . . ."

"Only what?" the Visser snapped.

"It belongs to the girl. If I kill the animal she will be angry. She may draw attention. Killing a cat is seen as a bad deed. It would violate my cover."

Visser Three did not look happy to be disobeyed. But he was not a creature who made impetuous decisions. He considered for a moment while my future just hung there, in the balance between life and death.

"Do not violate your cover or draw attention," the Visser said at last.

I figured it was time for me to do something in my own defence. I walked over and rubbed my flank against Chapman's leg.

"What is it doing?" Visser Three demanded.

"It is signalling that it wishes to be fed."

"Interesting. Claws and teeth and ferocity mixed with the subtlety to manipulate creatures larger than itself. A worthy creature. Yes, let it live, for now. Let it live until we have resolved the matter of the girl."

Chapman's face actually seemed to twitch. It was the only emotion he had shown, other than fear. "The girl? But . . . Visser . . . the agreement with the human Chapman . . ."

Visser Three sneered. "Agreements. Don't be a fool. We make agreements to gain voluntary hosts. Agreements are a tool. Just as you are my tool. If you had brought me the Andalite bandits, I would not have to concern myself with a cat or a girl."

Chapman bowed his head. "I will bring them to you."

"Do that," Visser Three said coldly. And then the solid-seeming image began to change. The gentle Andalite body melted away and in its place grew a monster like nothing ever seen on Earth.

Where the Andalite head had been, there was now a long, thick tube. There was an opening like some horrible mouth at the end of the tube. The thing was purple, but translucent. You could almost see through it, although I wasn't sure if that was because it was a hologram, or if the animal itself was that way.

The hologram Visser lowered the tube-mouth towards Chapman's head. The mouth opened, revealing hundreds, maybe thousands, of tiny suckers, each dripping slime.

It seemed as if the tube mouth closed over Chapman's head.

Chapman shook and quivered in terror.

Visser Three's artificial voice said, "Don't forget, Iniss two two six, I gave you this Chapman body. I placed you in his head because I trusted you. I fed you his brain and made you my lieutenant. But I can suck you back out again if you fail me. Would you like to see what happened to the last fool who failed me?"

Suddenly an image appeared in the air, like a little movie. It was a second hologram. It showed a human woman, pain-wracked, screaming, with the purple creature sucking on her head.

The real Chapman began to moan. "Oh, oh, no, Visser. I beg you."

In the little movie the translucent purple thing suddenly went into a spasm. From the woman's ear there came the slug. It was sucked, dripping, grey, slimy, right out of her head.

The purple creature swallowed the Yeerk slug.

Then the little movie ended.

"Not a very pretty picture, is it, Iniss two two six?"

Chapman just shook his head. His eyes were still staring at the empty air where the image had appeared.

Visser Three began to resume the Andalite form.

"Don't fail me," Visser Three said.

Chapter 14

Suddenly Visser Three vanished. The room was dark again. Chapman sat hunched over the desk, with his head in his hands. It was a while before he opened the door and we both went back up the stairs.

Ms Chapman was there, waiting. "What are the Visser's orders?" she asked in a whisper.

Chapman looked at her like he'd just seen a ghost. "He wants the Andalite bandits. He . . . he morphed into a Vanarx. A *Yeerkbane*." He kept his voice low, too. He glanced towards the stairs. I guess he was checking to see if Melissa was around.

Ms Chapman shuddered. "I'd heard that he

acquired a Vanarx. I always thought it was just another story to frighten his underlings."

"He showed me . . . he showed how he destroyed Iniss one seven four."

Ms Chapman looked shocked. "He used a Vanarx on an Iniss of the second century?"

"That Andalite-Controlling scum," Chapman said viciously. "I wish the Council of Thirteen *would* find out what kind of a mess he's making on this planet. Let them take that Andalite body from him and throw him back in some distant pool on the home world."

"Don't wish for that," Ms Chapman said grimly. "Long before Visser Three loses power, he will surely have destroyed you for failing him."

My cat ears noticed the sound before either of the Chapmans. Movement. Human feet pounding. I cocked my ears towards the stairs.

"Hey, Mum? Dad? Can one of you help me with this maths problem?"

It was Melissa. She was halfway down the stairs. She stopped and glanced hopefully at her parents. Or at least at the people who had once been her parents.

"We're busy right now, Melissa," Chapman snapped.

"Besides, dear, you should do your own work. That's how you learn," Ms Chapman said. "If you still can't figure it out later, your father will help you."

Melissa's face fell. She forced a smile, but there was no happiness there at all. "I guess you're right, Mum. It's just this square root stuff."

She hesitated, like she was hoping her that her parents might change their minds and go back upstairs with her.

Ms Chapman smiled. It was a smile as empty as Melissa's. "Square roots are hard to understand, aren't they? But I know you can do it."

"I'll come up and check on you before you turn in, sweetheart," Mr Chapman said.

The words were normal enough. I guess my own mum or dad could have said exactly the same things to me. "Dear." "Sweetheart." But the way they were said . . . There was something missing. Humanity. Love. Call it whatever you want. The words were right, but they were completely wrong.

It was horrible. Horrible in a totally different way than the monsters we had fought in the Yeerk pool. This was the kind of horrible that made you want to cry instead of scream.

And suddenly I found myself running after Melissa as she headed back up the stairs. When I reached her room, Melissa sat down on the bed and began sobbing.

<Rachel? Can you hear me?>

<Yes, Tobias. I'm up out of the basement. I'm upstairs in Melissa's room.>

<Thank goodness. I've been trying you every minute or so. I was worried that you were trapped downstairs.>

<No, I'm out.>

<Good. You have more than an hour left, but Fluffer is trying to head home. Cassie and Jake and Marco are trying to capture him again, but you know better than anyone how wily he can be.>

Melissa flopped on her face on the bed. She pulled a pillow over the back of her head and just cried.

<I can't leave just yet,> I said.

<Rachel, if the real Fluffer walks in while you're still there . . .>

<Yeah, I know. But I still can't leave right now. I have something I have to do.>

I went over to the bed. As small as I was, the side of the bed looked like a wall. It could have been the side of a two-storey building. I settled back on my haunches, gathering energy in my leg muscles. Then I sprang up, effortlessly, to land with perfect grace on the bed.

I walked over to Melissa and sniffed her hair sticking out from under the pillow. I heard a sound coming from somewhere. It was a sound that reminded me of my mother.

It reminded me of *both* my mothers, the human woman, and the cat who had licked my fur and carried me around in her mouth.

I recognized the sound. It was purring.

I was purring.

Melissa put her arm around me and drew me close. The physical contact made me a little anxious. It made the cat in me want to leave. But then she started scratching my neck and behind my ears. I purred a little louder and decided to stay for a while.

"I don't know what I've done," Melissa said.

It startled me to realize she was talking to me. Did she guess the truth? Did she know I was human?

No. She was just a girl talking to her cat.

"I don't know what I did," Melissa repeated. "Tell me, Fluffer McKitty. What did I do?"

<Rachel, what are you doing in there?>

<Tobias, I have plenty of time.>

<You have less than an hour. Don't push your luck. Jake is practically having a fit out here. He's telling me to tell you to get out.>

<Not yet. Melissa needs me.>

I had stopped purring. Probably because I was preoccupied, arguing with Tobias. I started purring again. I felt Melissa needed me to purr.

She was still crying. Still scratching slowly behind my ears.

"What did I do, Fluffer?" she asked again. "Why don't they love me any more?"

I felt like my own heart would break right then. Because I knew now why Melissa had stopped hanging out with me. I knew why she had become more withdrawn. And I knew how little hope there was for her.

My stomach turned and twisted.

Next time Marco asked why we were fighting the Yeerks, I knew I would have a whole new answer. Because they destroy the love of parents for their daughter. Because they made Melissa Chapman cry in her bed with no one to comfort her but a cat.

It was a small answer, I guess. I mean, it wasn't some high-sounding answer about the entire human race. It was just about this one girl. My friend. Whose heart was broken because her parents were no longer really her parents.

<Look, Rachel, I told Jake what you said. He said to remind you that you have a job to do in there. You're not in there to —>

<Tell Jake to shut up, Tobias,> I said angrily. <I'll come out. I'll come out. Just not yet.>

I purred as loud as I could. Melissa cried. And it came to me, like a vision: all the children all over, those whose parents had been made into Controllers. And the parents whose children had been taken from away them to be turned into

Controllers. It was a terrible image. I wondered how it must feel to see your parents stop loving you.

After a while, Melissa fell asleep. I got up and padded down the stairs to the pet door.

It was chilly outside. My friends were all waiting. They were also a little mad at me for making them wait and worry.

"You only have ten minutes to spare, Rachel," Jake said. "I hope it was worth scaring us all half to death. Did you at least discover something useful?"

<Yes. I discovered plenty. I discovered that Chapman has a way to communicate directly with Visser Three. I discovered that Visser Three is pretty hot to catch us, although he still thinks we're Andalites. And I *decided* something, too.>

"What?" Cassie asked me.

<I decided that I don't care what it takes, or how many risks I have to run. I don't care what happens to me. I hate these Yeerks. I hate them. I hate them. And I will find a way to stop them.>

Chapter 15

That night and the next morning, I barely got any homework done. In maths class that day I got the first "C" I'd got in a long time. My grades were starting to fall because I was busy trying to save the world. Or at least to save my old friend.

I knew now what had happened. Why Melissa and I weren't friends any more, at least not close friends. Something had gone terribly wrong in her life. Her parents no longer loved her. They pretended to, they sounded like they did, but Melissa knew it was all wrong.

Every time I thought of it, I felt like my insides were burning up from the anger. I guess I knew a little bit about what she was feeling.

When my parents got divorced, I worried that maybe that meant they didn't love me any more.

I was wrong. They still did. I don't see my dad as much as I would like to, but he does love me. My mum loves me. Even my sisters love me. Love is pretty important. It's a bit like wearing a suit of armour. It makes you strong.

On my way out of maths class, Jake came sidling up next to me. "Meeting later, OK?"

"Yeah. Whatever. Where at?"

"The church tower, where we were the other day."

"OK. But it's a long walk."

He turned around to face me, walking backward and grinning. "So, don't *walk*," he said. He waved and headed off down the hall.

Two hours later I was in the air. Let me tell you something: Getting that big eagle body off the ground isn't easy. It is definitely work. I wondered if my human body got any of the aerobic benefits of the exercise.

Once I got clear of the ground, I was able to catch little gusts of wind to climb higher. But it wasn't till I made it above the trees and the school buildings that I started getting a good, solid breeze that helped lift me up.

When I finally got high enough, I spotted Tobias. His reddish tail feathers were like a beacon.

<Man, that was a workout,> I said when I got close enough.

<Tell me about it. Follow me. The mall is an excellent place for thermals.>

<The mall? Why the mall?>

<It's all that parking space. See, the concrete gets hot in the sun. The concrete, the cars, the buildings themselves, they're all hot. So there's almost always a nice warm updraft.>

<Flying is like the nicest thing in the world,> I said dreamily.

<Yes, it is,> Tobias agreed. <One of the nicest things. But there are things you miss, too. Sitting back on the couch with a can of pop and a bag of chips and no school the next day and something good on TV. That's a good feeling, too.>

He didn't sound like he was feeling sorry for himself. Just like he was mentioning something that happened to be true.

<There's the church tower. I see another bird heading towards it. And I think I see Cassie coming out of her morph.>

<Down we go,> Tobias said.

Ten minutes later I had morphed back into my human body.

"You know what we need?" Marco said. "We need to coordinate these morphing outfits. I mean, Cassie's wearing green patterned leggings and a purple stretch top, and Jake's got on those awful bike shorts, and Rachel is stylish, as always, in her black tights. Put it all together and we look pretty scruffy."

"What do you want?" Jake asked him. "You want us all to wear blue with a big number four on our chests? Become the Fantastic Four?"

<The Fantastic Four *plus* the amazing Bird Boy,> Tobias added.

"No way," Marco said. "Not Fantastic Four. I'm thinking more an X-Men kind of thing. It's not about being identical, it's just about having some *style*. Right now, if anyone saw us, they wouldn't think 'Oh, cool, superheroes,' they'd think 'Man, those people do not know how to dress.'"

"Marco," I said, "I think it's time to get over this fantasy of yours. We are not superheroes. This is not a comic book."

"Yes, but I really, really want it to be a comic book. See, in a comic book the heroes don't get killed. I mean, OK, they killed Superman that time, but it was only temporary."

"Can we deal with reality here?" Jake asked. "We have business to discuss."

"What's the matter with combining green and purple?" Cassie asked Marco.

"It's a major fashion no-no," Marco said.

"Been reading *Vogue* again, Marco?" I teased.

Jake put his hand over Marco's mouth. "Okay people? And I use the term loosely. We need to decide what we're doing next."

Marco pried Jake's hand away. "I want to decide what we're *not* doing next. I should be spending more time with my dad. You know, he's still messed up over my mum. . . ."

Marco's voice always cracked whenever he mentioned his mum. He'd start out sounding tough and all, but his voice would end up with that little break, that little wobble. It had been two years since his mother disappeared. They said she drowned, although they never found her body. His father had fallen apart. It was the main reason Marco was so reluctant to be an Animorph. He was worried that if anything ever happened to him, his dad would just give up totally.

I could see that Jake was about to say something impatient. And I was feeling the same way, like Marco just needed to deal with reality.

But Cassie put her hand on Marco's arm. "Don't ever let any of this get in the way of spending time with your dad," she said earnestly. "He needs you. We need you, too, Marco, but your dad comes first." She looked at Jake, then at me. "There isn't much point in doing any of this if we forget *why* we're doing it."

I thought about Melissa. And I thought about my mum and dad and how great it was to have them, even when they got on my nerves.

"Cassie's right. When you get home, tell your dad you love him, Marco." I blurted it out without thinking about it. It wasn't the kind of thing I normally say.

"Thank you, Doctor Rachel," Marco said.

He said it snidely, but I could see he knew what I was talking about. Then he was suddenly all business. He rubbed his hands together. "OK, let's get serious here. How are we going to go about getting ourselves killed next? Turn into flies at a frog convention? Morph into turkeys at Thanksgiving?"

"I want to go back in," I said. "Back into Chapman's."

"Why?" Jake asked. "We learned a lot already. We —"

"We didn't learn the location of the Kandrona," I pointed out. "That's what we need to do, sooner or later. The Andalite made it pretty clear to Tobias that the Kandrona is the weak point for the Yeerks. The Kandrona sends out the rays that are concentrated in the Yeerk pools. If we destroy the Kandrona, we hurt them bad."

Marco raised a sceptical eyebrow. "Excuse me, Rachel, but what *is* a Kandrona? I mean, we know what it *does*, but what does it look like?

How big is it? For all we know, the Kandrona could be the size of a lighter and be in Visser Three's pocket."

<That's not the impression I got from the Andalite,> Tobias said.

"Whatever," Marco said impatiently. "The point is: How do we destroy something when we don't even know what it is?"

"That's why we have to follow the one lead we have," I said. "Chapman. Chapman communicates with Visser Three. The two of them know where the Kandrona is. If I can spy on them, maybe I can figure it out."

They were all staring at me. Marco looked at me like I was crazy. Jake looked thoughtful. Cassie looked worried, like she wasn't sure about what I was saying.

Tobias turned his fierce, intimidating hawk's stare on me. <Are you sure you're just going back to spy on Chapman?> he asked me privately.

"I don't think you should go back in there alone," Jake said.

"How is anyone else going to go in with me?" I asked. "We can't have *two* cats running around. I mean, as Fluffer I can go anywhere without any of them being suspicious."

See . . . I hadn't told anyone about Visser Three telling Chapman to kill me. I knew it was wrong to keep secrets like that from the group.

117

But if I'd told them, they would have never let me go back in.

Unfortunately, although Jake may not be all that perceptive, Cassie is.

"Are you *sure* nothing went wrong while you were in there, Rachel?" Cassie asked me. She was looking at me with this kind of sideways look Cassie gets when she's trying to figure someone out.

"It was scary," I said. "But nothing happened." It wasn't exactly a lie. Kind of a lie, but not exactly.

Cassie thought for a moment. Her eyes went blank. Suddenly I knew what was going on: Tobias was talking to her privately. He was telling her something. She nodded like she was agreeing.

Tobias didn't know what happened with Visser Three. But he did know that I was pretty freaky when I came up out of that basement.

"I think we should find a way for someone to go along with Rachel," Cassie suggested.

"What are you going to do, turn into a flea and ride on my back?" I asked her.

She smiled and gave a little shrug. "I'm just saying we should think about it."

"OK then," Jake said. "Rachel goes in one more time. Maybe we'll get lucky."

"We haven't got lucky since we walked through that construction site and met our first alien," Marco said.

"Maybe that's going to change," I said. "I'm going in and I'm finding a way to hurt those creeps."

<That's not the only reason you're going back in there,> Tobias said in my head. <You're not just doing it to hurt the Yeerks, you're going back in there because you want to help Melissa.>

"Same thing," I said. I guess the others wondered who I was talking to.

Chapter 16

It was a dark and stormy night.

Sorry, I've always wanted to write that. But it really *was* a dark and stormy night.

"Where is Jake?" I asked as we all got together down the street from Chapman's house. Everyone else was there. Cassie and Marco were wearing raincoats, although it hadn't started raining yet. Tobias was overhead, trying to hold on to a branch in a tree while the wind tried to knock him off.

"Jake had to stay home," Marco said. "Something about his dad grounding him."

"Why would his dad ground him?"

"How do I know?" Marco said, sounding

grouchy. "You know how parents are. Don't ask *me* to explain them."

I bit my lip. Somehow I felt more nervous with Jake being absent. The crazy wind whistling through the branches wasn't helping my confidence, either.

<I've spotted Fluffer,> Tobias said so all could hear. <He's kind of torturing a little rat he's found. But at least it's not a shrew.>

"Look, I'm not a big fan of shrews just because I sort of was one." I took a deep breath. "OK, look, we can't always count on all of us being together, I guess. So we go without Jake."

I glanced at Cassie. She smiled blandly. Something was going on with her, but I didn't have time to find out what.

<I'll scope out the area,> Tobias volunteered. He opened his wings a little and was immediately propelled out of the tree by the wind. I watched as he rode it expertly, swooping quickly up into the air beyond the range of my weak human eyes.

After a while we saw something shooting over our heads at about fifty miles an hour. <All clear,> Tobias called down as he shot past.

I felt strange. A little nauseous. A little scared. Everything seemed strange tonight. The weird thing was, I knew I'd feel better as soon as I morphed.

I concentrated. The first raindrop fell just as I felt my tail grow out behind me. By the time I had fallen to the ground, surrounded by the tent of my clothing, the rain had started for real.

"Oh, perfect," Marco said. "This just gets more and more fun."

<At least *you* have a raincoat,> I said. <I have nothing but fur. And this rain makes it impossible to smell anything out here.>

Cassie squatted next to me. She's just a normal-sized girl, but when you're a five-kilo cat any human being looks like Godzilla.

"Be careful, Rachel," Cassie said. And then she stroked my back. I started to move away, but she kept her hand on my back for a few seconds. Then, smiling mysteriously, she stood up.

I found I soon lost interest in Cassie's expression. Cats really don't have much interest in humans at all, unless food is involved.

<I'm out of here,> I said. I took off at a medium run. Cats don't like rain. I could feel the cat brain's distaste. I'd always thought cats hated all water. But that wasn't Fluffer's attitude. See, to him it was all about the smells and the sounds. Rain washes away scents. Without scents, a cat feels cut off and lost.

Almost as bad as losing smells is the fact that rain plopping all around you makes it harder to listen for the important sounds: the tiny high-pitched squeaks and the little furtive scritching noises.

Rain to cats is like being in the dark is to human beings. It just makes the whole world kind of boring.

So I ran towards the kitty door, actually looking forward to the friendly smells and sounds of home. At least, that's what Fluffer was thinking. I was still wondering why Jake hadn't come. And I was wondering if it was some kind of bad omen. There was a bad feeling over this whole mission.

I knew my way around the Chapman home, both as a cat and as a human. And I was pretty sure I knew the routine. Last time Visser Three had made contact right at eight o'clock. If Visser Three communicated with Chapman at the same time every night, then I had arrived right on schedule.

Chapman was sitting on the couch, same as last time. And just as I'd hoped, at three minutes to eight he stood up and headed down towards the basement.

My whole plan was to go down there with him. I remembered the layout of the little secret room. I remembered the desk. I knew if I could somehow follow him down without him seeing me and then get under the desk, I would be invisible to him, and to the Visser Three hologram.

The problem was that the whole plan counted on Chapman not noticing me.

He headed for the basement door. I fell into step right behind him. The trick was to stay just centimetres behind his feet. From there he couldn't see me. But I had to watch his feet closely. If he hesitated, I could plough right into him. That would be a very un-catlike thing to do.

He walked. I kept pace perfectly, just behind.

He headed down the stairs. I figured this part would be easier. When people walk down stairs they usually look where they are going. They don't turn around and look behind them.

But one sound, one clumsy move, and I was finished.

We reached the bottom of the stairs. Suddenly Chapman stopped dead.

I leaped behind the couch.

He looked around, like he'd heard a noise. Or maybe he just sensed something.

I froze. I didn't move a muscle.

He started on towards the door. I fell into step behind him again.

<So, what's happening?>

I nearly had a heart attack.

My tail puffed up. My back fur went straight up. I almost bolted.

Chapman stopped and I nearly got entangled

in his legs. His left foot moved. I dodged. He backed up a little. I squirmed out of the way.

<It's me, Jake. What's going on, Rachel?>

Jake?

Chapman opened the door of the secret room. He stepped through. I was right between his monstrously big feet. If he happened to glance down . . .

But he didn't. He didn't, and when he turned around to shut the door behind him, I bolted for the desk. I jammed my body as far back in the dark corner as I could.

I'd made it . . . barely. I was alive . . . so far.

<Rachel? Can you hear me?>

<Jake! Where are you? You scared me half to death.>

<Are we OK?> He sounded concerned.

Me, I was just angry.

<What do you MEAN are WE OK?> I yelled silently. <Where are you?>

<Well . . . I'm kind of on you.>

<*On* me? Jake, this is not the time to be playing jokes.>

Chapman sat down at the desk. His feet pushed beneath the desk, just narrowly missing me as I once again dodged nimbly out of the way.

<Sorry. I can't exactly see.>

I kept my eyes focused on Chapman's feet.

Cats have incredible powers of concentration. I focused hard on those big feet, each almost as big as I was. I had to stay out of their way. That was the key to staying alive.

<Jake, we're in kind of a situation here. In like ten words or less, where are you?>

<In ten words or less, I morphed,> Jake said. <I'm a flea.>

Chapter 17

<Excuse me?> It would have been real funny if I hadn't been so terrified. <Are you telling me you morphed into a flea? A *flea*?>

<Yeah. I'm on your back. Or your head. I can't tell. I don't really have eyes. At least not eyes that see anything I can understand. I mean, all I know is warm or not warm. I . . . I think I can sense blood. That's about it. And I can kind of sense motion. Like when your hair stood up, I knew there was something going on around me.>

<Jake, this is sick. This is beyond sick. What is the matter with you? A flea? Are you insane? Just being a lizard made you sick. This is way worse.>

<Actually, it's kind of OK,> he said. <I mean,

127

I don't know how to explain it, but the flea mind is so limited it's not hard at all to control. All it knows is to move towards the sense of warm blood, and eat. It's like . . . I don't know, like in a way I'm not even really in the flea because I can't see much or sense much. I expected it to be horrible, but when Cassie and Marco and I tested it out —"

<They're in on this with you?> Of course! That's why Cassie had made such a point of patting my head. She was depositing Jake on me.

<Rachel, we were worried about you. We figured someone should go along with you. Tobias said —>

<Ah, so Tobias is in on this, too.>

<Tobias said you were not telling us everything. He wasn't sure why, or what it was you weren't telling.>

I sighed inwardly. I guess it's good to have friends who care about you. But on the other hand, Jake had practically made me run into Chapman. Besides, the idea of Jake morphing into a flea and crawling around in my fur just gave me the worst creeps you can imagine.

Suddenly the brilliant light went on. Visser Three appeared in the room.

<Jake. The Visser is here in hologram. So don't distract me, OK? We're hiding under the

desk about a centimetre away from Chapman's foot.>

<Oh. But it doesn't matter if he sees you, right? I mean, he'll just figure you're the cat. No biggie. So you shouldn't be acting suspicious.>

I hesitated. Oh, well, it would have to come out sooner or later. <Um, Jake? That thing I didn't tell you? It's that Visser Three saw me in here last time. He told Chapman he should probably just . . . you know . . . kill me. He was worried I might be an Andalite in morph.>

For a while Jake didn't say anything. I had the feeling he was trying to keep himself from yelling at me. He failed.

<Rachel, are you CRAZY? You came back down here after that? Are you INSANE?>

But just then Chapman began to speak. "Welcome, Visser. Iniss two two six of the Sulp Niaar pool submits to you. May the Kandrona shine and strengthen you."

"And you," Visser Three said curtly. "Report."

"I have four new voluntary hosts, Visser," Chapman said. "Two are children recruited through The Sharing, the front organization. Of the two adults one is an agent for the FBI, a sort of policeman. He may be very —"

"FOOL!" Visser Three's artificial voice was flat, but still carried a load of anger. "Do I care about a handful of hosts? What have you learned of the Andalite bandits?"

"Visser, what can I do . . . unless they show themselves?"

"They used Earth animals in the attack on the pool," Visser Three said. "They used powerful, dangerous Earth animals. Find out how they obtained such morphs. My experts here tell me such animals are rare on this part of the planet."

"Yes, Visser. I will do —"

"Yes. You *will*. And we have another matter. We need six more human-Controllers, suitable for work as guards. They will be used to increase the guard around the Kandrona."

<What's happening?> Jake asked.

<Chapman is getting reamed by Visser Three.>

<Too bad Marco isn't here. He'd enjoy seeing Chapman get chewed out.>

<He wants us bad,> I said. <Or at least he wants the Andalites he thinks we are. He's putting extra guards around the Kandrona. Human-Controllers.>

<That's interesting, maybe he'll —>

The foot moved too quickly. The point of the shoe hit me in the ribs.

"Mrrrraaaoowwww!"

Chapman pushed back from the desk. He

passed right through the Visser Three hologram. For a second I saw them united, as if they were one horrible creature.

"What's happening?" Visser Three demanded.

Chapman stared at me, horror and fury in his eyes.

I flattened my ears back against my skull. My claws came out. My teeth were bared.

"It's the animal, Visser. The cat," Chapman said in a voice full of loathing and fear.

Visser Three seemed to make a seething, half-hissing noise.

"You should have killed it when I told you to, Iniss two two six."

"But Visser —" Chapman protested.

"And yet it all works out to my advantage," Visser Three said. "Now there can be no doubt that this cat is one of the Andalite bandits."

<Jake? We're busted,> I said. <We're busted really bad.>

"We will no longer have to search for the Andalites," Visser Three said. "We have one right here with us."

"Shall I kill it?" Chapman asked.

"No. Don't kill it. Seize it. Seize it now, before it can morph back into Andalite shape. By the time I am done with this one, we will have them all! It has been a long time since I tortured a proud Andalite warrior. But I know how to break them. Seize it and bring it to me!"

Chapman knew better than to argue.

Chapter 18

Chapman dived. His hands were open wide, grabbing for me.

I was trapped! No way out. No way to open that door and escape.

Trapped!

No sensible choice but to surrender.

But the cat and I were in agreement on this: You never surrender.

I felt my claws extend. My pupils were wide, ready to see every tiny movement. My ears were flattened back against my skull. My needle-sharp teeth were bared. My liquid steel muscles were coiled.

Chapman's hand seemed to slow down. It was like he was moving in slow motion. Everything seemed slower to my heightened cat senses. Only I was moving at normal speed.

My paw lashed out. My claws bit flesh. I saw three bright red tracks on the back of Chapman's hand.

I could smell the blood that flowed.

"Ahhhhh!" Chapman howled. He backed away.

"Get it!" Visser Three shouted.

<What's going on?> Jake wondered. <I feel like we're bouncing around a lot.>

Chapman got a determined look on his face. He came at me again. I was cornered. No way out.

I slashed. Chapman cried out.

My claws were lacerating him, tearing furrows in his arms and hands.

He grabbed me around the middle. The cat in me hated being grabbed that way.

Hated it a lot.

I brought my teeth into it. I was a five-kilo bundle of lightning-fast claws and teeth. Chapman's hands looked like raw hamburger.

"A magnificent animal!" Visser Three commented. "Twist it around. Hold it here with your forearm. That's right."

I did a lot of damage. Believe me, Chapman got hurt.

But in the end, no matter how tough I was, I

was just five kilogrammes of killer. Chapman was about eighteen times bigger.

He got his forearm around my chest. He had me pressed back against his chest. My front legs were pinned. With his other arm he managed to grab my hind legs.

All I could do was bite.

I bit. I bit again and again. But although I could hurt him, I couldn't kill him. I couldn't stop him. His fear of Visser Three was greater than the pain I was causing.

"Bring it to me," Visser Three said enthusiastically. "Bring it to me. I will come to collect it at the nearest landing site."

"Visser, what if it . . . Owww! . . . What if it resumes its Andalite shape?"

"You have weapons. If it tries to remorph, kill it."

"Yes . . . Ahhhh! . . . Rotten little beast! Yes, Visser. I will go directly."

"We will deal with this Andalite bandit. And bring the girl, too."

"The girl . . . Melissa?" Chapman asked.

"I have been indulgent for too long. This Andalite spy has penetrated your home. It is because of the girl. I have already chosen the Yeerk for her. Bring her with the Andalite. Obey me, Iniss two two six. Or prepare to face the Vanarx."

Visser Three's hologram disappeared. Chapman suddenly threw me across the room. I twisted in midair and brought my legs around for the landing. I hit the floor and skidded.

<OK, something is definitely going on out there.>

By the time I was up, Chapman had reached his desk and opened a drawer. His bloody hand came out with a small pistol-like device I had seen before. It was a handheld Dracon beam.

Chapman levelled the weapon at me. He was shaking. His face seemed to be twitching. The weapon jerked a little with each spasm. But I knew he would still have got me if I had tried to move.

<Are you going to tell me what's going on?> Jake demanded. <A few seconds ago I felt another warm body close by. And I think I'm sensing blood.>

<We're in kind of a mess,> I said.

<What kind of a mess?> Jake asked.

<Chapman has a Dracon beam pointed at me. He knows I'm not exactly a cat. He thinks I'm an Andalite. He's taking me to Visser Three.>

<Oh. This is bad.>

<It gets worse. Visser Three wants Melissa, too.>

Chapman opened the door a crack. "Get down here! Now!" he yelled upstairs.

I guess he saw my eyes flick towards the door. He made a fierce, vicious grin. "Try it, Andalite. Go ahead and try it. I'd love the excuse to fry you."

I decided not to head for the door.

"You've made life very difficult for me," Chapman said. "Very difficult. If I have to let Visser Three take the girl, my host will make life annoying for me. Do you know how tiring it is to have an uncooperative host? No, of course you don't. But trust me, Andalite: I will gladly kill you."

Ms Chapman appeared at the door. "What is it?"

"This cat is one of the Andalite bandits in a morph. Visser Three wants him. Get me the cage we use to take him to the vet."

Ms Chapman nodded and disappeared.

<What's going on now?> Jake asked.

<Ms Chapman is getting a cage,> I said. I was feeling utterly defeated. Because of me, the Yeerks were going to take Melissa. I had failed. I had made a mess of things.

Ms Chapman brought the cage. She opened the little barred door.

"In," Chapman snapped.

I didn't move.

"In," he said in a cruel whisper. "In or I'll finish you right here."

He looked like he meant it. I walked into the

137

cage. Ms Chapman closed the door and made sure it was locked.

Chapman snatched up the cage and carried me to the top of the stairs. "Now," he snapped at his wife, "go get . . . ungh!"

Peering through the slats in the side of the cage, I saw him stagger. His face was twitching like he was a crazy man. He seemed to be having a hard time getting control of his mouth. "Go . . . get . . . the . . . girl," he said through gritted teeth.

Ms Chapman started to obey, but then Chapman cried out.

"Oh! Ungh!" He fell to his knees. "He is . . . urgh . . . he is . . . fighting me. . . ."

"Host rebellion," Ms Chapman muttered under her breath. She seemed horrified and fascinated all at once. Then, suddenly, her left hand slapped her own face.

"Ahhhhh! Mine . . . mine . . . too."

"Stop it, Chapman," Chapman said. "Stop it or I'll break you! I'll leave you nothing but a shell! You cannot win. No host has ever succeeded in rebelling!"

But the Chapman host wasn't giving up.

It was terrible. Terrible in a way that made you want to watch. To anyone else it would have just looked as if our assistant principal and his wife were nuts. Chapman was talking to himself and twitching and contorting, still unable to get to his feet.

<The hosts are fighting the Yeerks!> I told Jake. <The human brains are resisting. Chapman is out of control. Ms Chapman is trying to choke herself with her own hand. The Yeerk is trying to regain control. It's incredible!>

<I can't believe it! I can't believe the hosts can fight back this hard.>

<It's because of Melissa. They're fighting for their daughter.>

"Aaaarrrrggh!" Chapman cried. Suddenly he lurched to his feet. "I will win, Chapman. You cannot resist!"

And it was true. The Chapman host was losing. Iniss two two six was regaining control.

The same was happening with Ms Chapman. The Yeerk in her head was forcing the rebellious hand away from her throat.

But neither of the Chapmans looked good.

<They're exhausted,> I reported to Jake. <They're regaining control, but they're both a mess. Sweating. Pale. Still trembling and jerking.>

Chapman looked at his wife. Or at least the Yeerk slug in Chapman's brain ordered his eyes to look towards the body that was controlled by a different Yeerk. It was harder now to think of Chapman as just being Chapman. I had seen proof that there were two creatures inside him.

I even knew what that was like. There were two people in my head as well. I had fought to control the shrew, just as the Chapman Yeerk now fought to control Chapman's brain.

Chapman said, "I have control again."

Ms Chapman nodded. "Yes. But just barely. They fight fiercely for their children, these humans."

"And they will not stop fighting. I can't maintain my cover with this host waiting to attack at every opportunity. I have to be at the school every day. The host is beaten and exhausted for now, but in a few days he will strike again." Chapman sounded angry and frustrated. "He's not a fool. He knows he can't win . . . he knows each battle will leave him weaker and that eventually I will triumph."

Ms Chapman kicked my cage, like it was all my fault. "He doesn't have to win. All he has to do is wait until you are in a meeting with parents or members of the school board, then strike. They'll think you've lost your mind."

Chapman looked haunted. He checked his watch. "I'll take the Andalite to Visser Three. Maybe . . . maybe I can make him understand."

"Go, quickly," Ms Chapman told him.

Chapman snatched up the cage I was in. He barrelled through the door. He slammed me into the doorjamb on the way.

"Daddy? Daddy? What are you doing?"

It was Melissa. She was across the living room. I hadn't seen her arrive. Where had she been? I could only pray that she had not heard everything. If she'd heard it all, there was no hope for her.

Chapman kept walking. Out into the wet night.

"Daddy? Do you have Fluffer in there?"

<It's Melissa,> I told Jake. <If she doesn't back off, she's going to force them to take her!>

"Daddy?" Melissa sounded frightened now. She came running. Chapman moved quicker. The real Chapman was helping. He knew his daughter would only make things worse if she tried to intervene.

"Fluffer!" Melissa cried.

There was only one hope. <Tobias?> I cried out, making my thought-speech as loud as I could. <Tobias, can you hear me?>

His answer was faint, but it was Tobias. <Yes, Rachel.>

<The real Fluffer! We need him. We need him right now!>

<Rachel, what is going on out there?> Jake demanded.

"Fluffer! Why are you taking Fluffer? Daddy, stop!"

Chapter 19

Out the front door we went. Out into the night. Melissa, sobbing pitifully. Jake, demanding to know what was happening. Chapman, walking as fast as he could.

Melissa grabbed her father's arm. The cage wobbled wildly.

"Daddy, you can't take Fluffer. Don't take him away! What are you doing?"

The car. I could see it in the driveway. We were almost there.

Suddenly, I heard a yowling, yammering, high-pitched sound that started as a hiss and ended as a shriek.

Like a bullet he came, racing across the lawn.

The *real* Fluffer.

He was running like every monster in the world was right behind him.

In the darkness the humans couldn't see what was scaring Fluffer so badly. But with my cat eyes I could see perfectly. Just a few metres off the ground, like some dark shadow of death, came Tobias.

Fluffer must have recognized his cage. He must have figured that if he just got inside he'd be safe from the talons of the raptor that pursued him.

Fluffer leaped towards the cage. He glommed on to it and tried to dig his claws into the plastic.

For one frozen instant Fluffer McKitty saw something he never expected to see. Fluffer saw himself.

It was almost as weird for me. The cat in my head was totally baffled. This new cat smelled exactly like himself. This did not make any sense at all. It meant nothing. It wasn't even a part of any cat reality. The human part of me noticed a small cut on Fluffer's head. Tobias had taken a good swipe at him to get him moving in the right direction.

"Fluffer?" Melissa said. "But . . ." She tried to peer inside the cage.

Chapman was quick. "No, sweetheart," he said. "This isn't Fluffer at all. It's some other cat that sneaked into the basement. He's different. I'm taking him to the shelter so his owners can pick him up."

"But why didn't you just tell me that?"

Chapman looked confused. "I . . . I didn't notice you."

Melissa stepped back like she'd been slapped. "But Daddy, I was crying."

"Sorry." Chapman shrugged. He shoved the cage into the backseat.

We drove off. I breathed a sigh of relief. I knew Melissa wasn't safe yet, but she was safe for now, at least.

<Good work, Tobias,> I said. But I don't think he could hear me. And I couldn't see out of the windows, so I didn't know if he or Marco or Cassie were anywhere close.

<Jake? You still with me?>

<Yes. Do you have a minute to fill me in? This flea existence is fine for hiding, but I can't tell anything about what's going on.>

<I'm in a cat carrier. Chapman's in the front seat. He watches me through the rearview mirror. He still has the Dracon beam. I think maybe I'm in pretty big trouble here.>

<We're not beaten yet,> Jake said.

<Jake, time must be getting short. It's been at least an hour. You must have morphed before me. You need to get away and morph back.>

<We still have time,> Jake said.

<You have a watch, Jake?> I asked. <I don't think so. You're what, about twice the size of a full stop on the page of a book? You can't risk being trapped in a flea morph. Besides, there's nothing you can do.>

We hadn't travelled far before the car started bouncing and rattling over rough road.

<As soon as we get outside you need to jump off, Jake,> I said. <Just make yourself jump *away* from warmth and away from the smell of blood. You can do that.>

The car came to a stop.

<Rachel, there is no way I'm going to leave you alone.>

I knew he was trying to be brave, but he was making me mad. <Jake, we're trapped. He's got a Dracon beam and I'm in a cage. Visser Three is coming to get me. I can't morph back or they'll see I'm human. Chapman will recognize me. How long do you think it will take them to figure out who the rest of us are? It would be the end of us all. The end of the Animorphs. The end of the only hope for stopping these guys. Come on, Jake, you know it's true.>

<We're not beaten yet,> Jake repeated stubbornly.

<The only hope is for me to stay in cat morph,> I said. <They'll probably . . . you

146

know . . . but at least they'll never find out about the rest of you. Now jump off me.>

Chapman got out of the car. He came around and opened the back door.

"Time to meet the Visser, Andalite. He'll have a wonderful time with you."

Chapman lifted me out of the backseat. I looked out through the bars.

<We're at the construction site,> I told Jake. <Now get off me.>

<I'm not —>

I couldn't argue with Jake any more. I was afraid now. Afraid. I could picture what Visser Three might do to me.

<Sorry, Jake, but this time I'm the boss,> I said. I cocked my rear leg and started scratching in that rapid catlike way.

<What the . . . what are you doing?>

<I'm scratching. I want you off me.>

<OK, OK,> Jake said. <Just stop it. It's like an earthquake here. OK, Rachel. You're right. We've lost this battle.>

Chapman carried the cage into the construction site. I could see the ground go by beneath me. I could see through the bars all the half-built cinderblock buildings. I could see the very spot where the five of us had cowered in terror while Visser Three had morphed into a monster and swallowed the Andalite prince.

147

The Andalite's last despairing cry came back to me. He had lost his fight. Now I was losing mine.

Maybe there was no hope. Maybe we were fools to even try and resist the Yeerks.

<Get out of here, Jake,> I said.

<OK, Rachel. Here I go. Look . . . be strong, Rachel.>

<Yeah, Jake. You too.>

<Jumping . . .>

A few seconds later, Chapman put me down on the ground. He waited beside the cage. The two of us stared off into the darkness.

I decided to make sure Jake was gone. <Jake? Jake?>

No answer.

<Jake, answer me. I've changed my mind. I want you to stay with me.> If he had lied to me, he would answer now. <Come on, Jake, I've changed my mind. I need you.>

No answer. He was truly gone. That fact filled me with grim satisfaction. If Jake and the others survived, there would still be some hope.

But the feeling of loneliness was awful.

Then I heard the sound of something large, moving swiftly in the air. I pressed my head against the door and looked up. Three craft were descending towards the construction site.

Two of them were smaller, about the size of

one of those recreational vehicles, maybe a little larger. They had a cowled, insect-like look. They looked like beetles with twin long, serrated spears pointed forward on each side. The Andalite had called them Bug fighters.

The third craft was much larger, shaped like an angular battle-axe. It was black on black, sharp, and deadly looking. As it sank slowly towards us I felt my fear grow.

It was not the cat that was afraid. It was me, the human. The cat didn't know what this ship was. I did. I had seen it before. The Andalite had called it a Blade ship.

It was the personal ship of Visser Three. And terror seemed to flow from it. I could smell the fear sweat on Chapman.

I guess I was glad he was scared, too. Maybe Visser Three would become the Vanarx and suck the Chapman Yeerk out of Chapman's head. Maybe the true Chapman would experience a few seconds of freedom before he was killed. Maybe the Chapman Yeerk would suffer before Visser Three finished him off.

Maybe.

Fear is like a worm inside you. It eats you. It chews your guts. It bores holes in your heart. It makes you feel hollow. Empty. Alone.

Fear.

The Blade ship landed between two half-finished buildings. The Bug fighters came to rest on either side. They looked so strange, parked between the yellow-painted earthmovers and graders in the construction site.

The earthmovers looked like toys. The alien craft looked like deadly weapons.

I was afraid. I tried to borrow the cat's courage, his indifference. But then the door of the Blade ship opened. I had no courage.

Only fear.

Chapter 20

Visser Three in person is worse than Visser Three as a hologram. There's nothing horrible about him. Not when he's in his normal Andalite body, at least. Andalites are strange-looking, that's for sure. But they aren't frightening.

But I had met a real Andalite. You could feel the difference between a real Andalite and the evil beast that was Visser Three. It was like he glowed with some dark light. A light that cast a shadow over your mind.

Visser Three. Even Chapman feared him.

By the Visser stood two Hork-Bajir guards. Each was holding a Dracon beam, not that Hork-Bajir ever looked like they needed weapons. They *were* weapons. Marco had called them walking

Salad Shooters. They were living razor blades. Wickedly curved blades raked forward from their foreheads. More blades were at their elbows and wrists. Their feet were like Tobias's talons, only much bigger, like Tyrannosaur feet.

They were at least two metres tall, maybe a little more, with a spiked tail. The Andalite had told us that the Hork-Bajir were a good people, enslaved by the Yeerks, just the same way the Yeerks wanted to enslave humans. But it was hard to look at a Hork-Bajir and think they had ever been anything but killing machines.

Behind the Hork-Bajir came four Taxxons.

Imagine a centipede. Now imagine a centipede twice the length of a man and just as big around. Imagine that the centipede holds the upper third of its body erect. Imagine pointed legs like steel pins below, and smaller legs with little claws as you get closer to the head. Not that it has a real head. There are four separate globs that look like chopped-up red jelly that are the Taxxon's eyes. And at the very top, a mouth. The mouth is perfectly round and lined with row after row of small, needle teeth.

The Andalite told us that the Taxxons are all voluntary hosts. They are allies of the Yeerks.

And yet, as horrible as the Hork-Bajir and the

Taxxons were, it was Visser Three who made your skin crawl.

Without the hologram communicator, the Visser communicated in the usual Andalite fashion. He thought-spoke, much like we all did when we were in morph.

<That is the Andalite bandit?> he asked Chapman.

"Yes, Visser."

Visser Three advanced towards me, almost mincing on his delicate Andalite legs, looking like a cross between a deer, a human, and a scorpion. He aimed his main eyes at me. His stalk eyes scanned the area, always watchful. He brought his face close to the cage.

I was staring right into his face. I could see the nose slits open and close as he breathed. I could see the large, almond-shaped eyes narrow as he peered inside to get a better look at me.

He was only centimetres away. I should have tried to reach through the bars and at least bloody him a little.

But the fear was all over me. I was sick with terror. I'm not ashamed to admit it. I couldn't stand his eyes watching me. I turned away, afraid to look.

<Not so brave now, my Andalite friend?> Visser Three asked.

It was the first time any of us had ever been spoken to directly by the Visser. His voice was in my head, threatening and cruel and foul beyond description. It was a voice full of power — and hate. When he called me an Andalite, I almost burst out, "No, no, Visser, not an Andalite. A human. A human!"

It was like I could feel the terrible force of his will battering me. In an instant I knew: I would never survive his questioning. I would tell him everything. His power was a million times greater than mine. His will was a vast, huge, irresistible thing. And what was I? Just some foolish little girl. A foolish, lost girl. Lost.

And yet, even as I felt my own mind wither before the black terror of Visser Three, another mind came forward.

I was not alone. There was another in my head with me. Someone whose species memory had no images of Visser Three. Fluffer. Fluffer's mind contained fears, but they were different from my fears. Fluffer feared big predator birds. Fluffer feared loud aggressive dogs. Fluffer feared dominant male cats.

But Fluffer was not at all impressed by Visser Three.

On the edge of absolute panic, I let the cat in my mind take over. I sank back, hiding behind the calm cat brain.

Visser Three took the cage from Chapman. He lifted it up so he could see inside better.

And what did I do? What did Fluffer do? He stuck his little pink nose up against the bars and sniffed the air.

Fluffer wanted to find out what this creature was, and that meant getting a good smell of him.

<This is similar to the orange-and-black creature that invaded the pool,> Visser Three said.

It took me a second to track on this. Then I realized: he meant Jake. Jake had been in his tiger morph when we battled in the Yeerk pool.

"Yes, Visser," Chapman said. "They are a family of animals. Felines. These are the smallest."

<I see you damaged my servant Iniss two two six, Andalite,> Visser Three said to me. <No one ever accused you Andalites of lacking courage. You are a race of fools, but brave.>

What was I supposed to say? Thank you?

<Why not answer me, Andalite? I know you hear my words. This charade is pointless. I know what you are.>

I said nothing. I tried to think nothing. I was afraid that if I said anything at all he would instantly know I was not an Andalite. And if he realized I was human . . . the others would never be safe.

155

I had to stay in this body.

I had to die in this body, and take my secret with me.

Visser Three put my cage back down. <Now. Where is the girl? I have promised her to Iniss four five five. Iniss four five five is a spawn mate of yours, I believe. We will do the infestation aboard the mother ship, and I will have the girl returned tomorrow. Where is she?>

"Visser . . . I . . ." Chapman said.

The mask of politeness dropped from Visser Three in a microsecond. Even my cat eyes could barely follow his movements, they were so swift. Visser Three grabbed Chapman around the neck. His Andalite tail arched forward. The dagger point of the tail was in Chapman's face.

<Do you defy me?> It was like a hiss. The hiss of a snake.

"N-n-n-o, no, Visser." Chapman was shaking like a leaf. "I would never defy you. It's only . . . the host. Chapman. He and the woman rebelled."

<Aren't you able to control your host?> Visser Three sneered. <Do you think the Andalite mind that still lives in this body never resists? Do you imagine that your human host is more powerful than my own Andalite host?"

This wasn't going very well for Chapman. Not for the real, human Chapman, nor the human-Controller that called itself Chapman.

"Visser, I . . . I only report the facts to you. M-m-my host is under control. But I am constantly in contact with humans. I occupy a responsible position in their society. I cannot have my host body causing me to twitch and shake. Humans see such things as signs of mental illness. I could lose my position. And I would no longer be of any use to you."

<You are barely of use to me now,> Visser Three sneered.

"Visser, my host begs leave to address you directly," Chapman said.

Visser Three hesitated. I saw his stalk eyes scanning around, checking for any signs of threat. Instinctively I looked around, too. I had no way of knowing how well Visser Three's borrowed Andalite eyes could see in the dark. But for me the darkness was no barrier.

I looked. I didn't even know what I was looking for. But all I saw were the Hork-Bajir and the Taxxons, the Yeerk ships, silent and dark, and the buildings and forlorn construction equipment of the site.

Then I caught a glimpse of movement. It was in the woods that bordered the construction site. A swift side-to-side movement, just the sort of thing my cat eyes noticed best. But when I stared closer, I saw no further movement. Probably just another Hork-Bajir patrolling.

<I will allow the host to address me,> Visser Three said.

I craned my head up as well as I could to watch. For a moment, nothing changed. Then, suddenly, Chapman sagged. It was like he was a marionette and someone had cut his strings. He collapsed, straight down. His legs just twisted up under him.

He tried to stand up. But it was as if he didn't know how to make his legs work. They would jerk and suddenly kick out, but he could not stand. Finally, he gave up.

"Fisher," he mumbled. "Fisher Hree. Sor . . . I . . . sorry. Visher. Visser. Visser Three."

The real, human Chapman had been out of control of his own body for so long he no longer remembered how to move or speak.

"Visser Three," he said again. His voice was slurry and strange.

<Speak, you fool,> Visser Three snapped. <Do you think I can stay here forever?>

"Visser Three. You . . . We had a deal. You know I never wanted to join you. My wife did. But I said no. But . . . but then my wife . . . no longer my wife by then, of course." Suddenly he began to cry. I could see his tears very clearly. "My wife who was no longer my wife . . . my wife who was one of your creatures . . . threatened . . . threatened to give you my daughter."

Chapman managed to raise one clumsy hand to his eyes. "I forgive her. She was weak. And you feed on weakness."

<Yes, yes, get to the point,> Visser Three said.

A Hork-Bajir moved closer. He muttered something to the Visser, then moved away. I couldn't hear or understand what the Hork-Bajir had said, but it looked as if he was reminding Visser Three that they shouldn't hang around too long.

"The point is," Chapman said, "that I agreed to be made into a host. I agreed to . . . to . . ." He looked like he was about to throw up. "I agreed to surrender my freedom. To become a Controller. To accept this filthy thing in my head. To accept your control. I agreed . . . but only if you would spare my daughter."

It felt like my heart had stopped beating. Chapman had become a Controller to save Melissa? He had given more than his life to save his daughter?

<The situation has changed,> Visser Three said. <The Chapman person is an important part of our work. We cannot have him endangered by some uncontrollable human.>

"The girl — Melissa — is no threat. But . . ." Chapman struggled to lift himself up once again with clumsy legs and awkward arms. He rose to his knees. Then slowly, slowly, he stood up. He was wobbling and swaying, but he was standing.

"The girl is no threat," he repeated in a stronger, more confident voice. "But I am."

Chapter 21

<You? A threat?> Visser Three laughed. He reached out with one hand to push lightly on Chapman's chest. Chapman fell back, sprawled out on the dirt. His head was just centimetres from the door of my cage. Tears were streaming down the side of his face.

"If you harm my daughter I will fight you. I will fight you forever. Ask your Yeerk if he believes me. He knows me better than anyone. Ask Iniss two two six if I will fight for my daughter."

Chapman closed his eyes. The tears stopped. Then his eyes opened again. He picked himself up quickly from the ground and stood before Visser Three. The Yeerk slug was in charge again. He was once again a Controller.

Before he stood, I saw something that frightened me all over again. It was Chapman's watch. The time was now nine twenty-eight. I had about seventeen minutes before I hit the two-hour limit!

<The host will attempt to disrupt you?>

"Yes, Visser. And the woman as well. She is not as strong as this one, but she was able to gain control of one hand. Perhaps she has deeper strengths than we knew." He hesitated before going on. I could still smell the fear on him. "I am of more use with a passive, voluntary host. But I am your tool, Visser. I will do as you command."

<Yes, you will certainly do as I command,> Visser Three said. <But you have brought me the Andalite bandit.> He nodded down at me. <And this will occupy my time for a little while. Leave the girl, for now. Now get out of here. You tempt my patience.>

Chapman didn't need a second invitation. He jumped in the car and tore out of there.

Melissa was safe. As safe as she would ever be with Chapman as her father. That was something. Not much, but something.

<Move out,> Visser Three yelled. I saw the Hork-Bajir respond instantly to his command. The nearest one snatched me up and suddenly we were moving fast towards the Blade ship.

In seconds it would all be over. I would be aboard the Visser's ship. I would leave Earth. The only thing in my future was pain. Maybe I would die before I betrayed my friends. A depressing kind of thing to hope for.

<So. What's happening now?>

"*Mrrraaaoww!*" I jumped and spun around inside my cage. <Jake? Is that you?>

<Who else would it be? You know anyone else who would be a talking flea riding on your back?>

<Jake, you were supposed to get away and be safe!>

<Yeah, right. Like I was going to abandon you. Listen, I could hear Visser Three's thought-speech, but I don't know where we are.>

<We are about three metres away from being loaded into Visser Three's Blade ship. And I have about fifteen minutes left before I'm trapped in this morph.>

<Fifteen minutes? Great, if you have fifteen, I have ten. I had to morph earlier than you, remember.>

<Jake, get out of here! You can't be trapped as a flea!>

The door of the Blade ship slid open silently. I could see dark red light inside. I could see a handful of Taxxons that seemed to be standing over control panels of some sort. Hork-Bajir stood at attention.

163

<I'm not getting out of here,> Jake said. <None of us are.>

<None of . . . You mean the rest are fleas, too?>

<No, but they should be around somewhere. Tobias was supposed to follow us and lead the others to wherever we ended up.>

<They can't do anything.>

<Oh, really? Well, I bet they'll try.>

Just at that moment I heard a strange sound. My cat brain didn't recognize it. But the human me did. It was an engine. A big engine. Like a big truck. Or maybe a tractor. Or —

An earthmover.

The Hork-Bajir carrying me saw it, too. He ran into the Blade ship and tossed me down. Then he ran back to the Visser, who waited in the doorway.

<I think they've started one of the earth-movers,> I told Jake.

<Then I guess it's time for me to get into this fight,> Jake said. <I'm going to try a quick double-morph. Hope it works. Here goes nothing. Yeeee-haaah!>

All at once, through the open door of the Blade ship, I spotted the earthmover. It lumbered at a painfully slow speed. But it lumbered right towards the Blade ship.

<Get us into the air!> Visser Three shouted.

The nearest Taxxon said something in their slithery snake-speech. It sounded like "Sssree shway snerp snerrrup ssreet."

<Two minutes to liftoff? Too long!> Visser Three said. His tail whipped forward. I saw a huge gash open in the flesh of the Taxxon. Greenish-yellow goo poured out.

The other Taxxons all looked kind of excited. They were waving their little upper arms and snapping their little claws.

<You and you.> Visser Three pointed at two of the Taxxons. <Get us off the ground! The rest of you may feed on this fool.>

The wounded Taxxon emitted a wailing, slithery scream. Three other Taxxons rushed at him. Their circular mouths fastened on to their fellow Taxxon's writhing flesh and began chewing and tearing at him.

The sound of the diesel engine grew louder. Visser Three was rapping out orders. Hork-Bajir ran through the door and back outside.

Then I saw something happening in the dark corner of the cabin, over past the horrific Taxxon feeding frenzy. Something was growing. A human being was growing out of nothing.

<Jake!>

<Can't talk. Don't distract me.>

Visser Three was in a rage. You could feel the waves of his anger radiating around the small space. <Destroy that machine!> he ordered.

Outside, two Hork-Bajir took aim at the five tons of slow-moving steel.

Jake was still cowering in the corner, but he had begun to change once again. In the darkness my cat eyes could see the beginning of a pattern of stripes. Black and orange. The stripes of a tiger.

It was time for me to do my part. I concentrated. I felt the change begin. The cage grew small around me.

Rumble rumble rumble. The earthmover closed in.

The near-dead Taxxon screamed as his fellow Taxxons ate him alive.

Suddenly I saw a brilliant red light. There was a sizzling sound. I saw the earthmover disintegrate. My heart was in my throat. Marco! Cassie! Had they got away?

I had to concentrate. I had to ignore the Taxxon's screams. I had to stop wondering whether Cassie and Marco had been on that earthmover when it was hit. I had to control my morph. Not too far, Rachel. Not too much. I could *not* become human. Not totally human. I looked down at my paw. Short stubby fingers had appeared. I stuck these stubby half-human fingers through the bars of the cage and found the lock.

One of the feeding Taxxons looked away from his meal just long enough. "Yeerss srenn sssseeere!" It waved its creepy front legs in my direction.

Visser Three snapped around and glared at me with ferocious hatred.

I opened the door of my cage.

"Rrrrraaawwwrrr!" Jake leaped through the air, his huge claws outstretched.

I flew out of the cage, a clumsy mass of fur and skin, a creature that was half-cat and half-human.

Jake hit Visser Three in the side. <This time, you're *mine*, you jerk!>

Visser Three fell over, tangled up in tiger. His deadly tail flashed but missed. Jake ripped the Visser's flesh with claws infinitely bigger than mine.

<Aaaaarrrgghhh!>

It was a great pleasure hearing Visser Three scream that way. But I had other things to worry about.

I could hardly move in my half-morph. I concentrated on regaining my cat form. I had only minutes left before the two hours would be up.

Jake rolled off Visser Three just as a handful of Hork-Bajir rushed to the Visser's defence.

<Run!> Jake yelled.

167

<Run!> I agreed.

We ran. I was back fully in Fluffer's shape. I could do fifty kilometres an hour, as fast as the fastest human being could run.

Unfortunately, Hork-Bajir are faster.

Jake was faster still, for short distances. Fast enough to outrun the Hork-Bajir that were after us. But he wasn't going to leave me behind.

Jake turned and came for the closest Hork-Bajir.

I saw him flying over my head, a huge beast, orange-and-black striped. The Hork-Bajir went down hard. <Get outta here, Rachel! You're too small to fight these guys.>

But there was still another Hork-Bajir on my tail. Faster than me. Too fast!

I dodged left. The Hork-Bajir shot past me. I turned back sharply, my little pads scrabbling in the dirt. The Hork-Bajir grabbed for me but missed.

Something else was moving. Something big. The ground was rumbling. . . .

A second earthmover was grinding forward on its tank treads. Marco and Cassie had started up another earthmover!

I raced towards the nearest half-finished building. I had to get away. And I had to morph back. Time was up. In minutes I would be trapped!

I saw a dark hole. I flew towards it in a single leap. The hole led under a wall. Then it opened into a shallow basement. There was a concrete floor less than a metre over my head. I was safe! Safe, and with room enough to morph back to human shape.

I tried to concentrate. Out beyond my little concrete shelter I heard growls and alien cries. I heard the rumble of the earthmover. I thought I heard the sizzle of Dracon beams.

Human, I told myself. Return to human. Only minutes left!

Then I felt a shattering noise. Then another. It was like some giant was stomping around.

The giant steps stopped. I was frozen, unable to even think, let alone morph.

Crash!

All around me pillars of rock-hard, scaled flesh, each as big around as a tree trunk, ripped into the concrete.

Grrrunch!

The concrete was lifted off me. Torn away, like it was paper.

I was exposed. Trapped. And standing over me, with the shattered concrete floor in its mighty hand, was a beast that seemed to be made of living rock.

<You won't get away so easily,> Visser Three said.

Chapter 22

It was all over. I knew I was done for. Nothing in the world could stop the beast Visser Three had morphed into.

He was seven metres tall. As tall as a telephone pole. He stood on three massive legs, each as big around as a redwood tree. He had a tiny head, not much bigger than a human head. He would have looked funny, except that there was nothing funny about what he was doing.

With two long, mighty arms he was casually tearing up the concrete. He slammed his fingers into the cement. He ripped it up in slabs and tossed them over his shoulder.

One of the slabs hit a Hork-Bajir and crushed

him. I don't think Visser Three even noticed or cared.

I ran.

Crash! One of the Visser's huge hands slammed down in front of me.

I scampered back and turned.

Crash! Another hand like living rock slammed in front of me.

Even the cat in me knew — it was hopeless.

Visser Three glared down at me with tiny bright eyes in that weirdly small head. He reached for me with both hands, cupped together, forming a wall around me.

C-R-R-R-U-N-C-H!

Visser Three hesitated.

B-O-O-O-O-M!

I bolted.

I leaped to the top of a wall. Two metres straight up, and trust me, as scared as I was, I could have jumped even higher.

Out of the corner of my eye I saw what had happened. The earthmover had ground forward and slammed into one of the Bug fighters. The Bug fighter had exploded.

<AAAAAAARRRRRRGGGHHH!> Visser Three roared in fury. I did not envy the Hork-Bajir and Taxxons who had let that earthmover get through.

I ran along the top of that wall. Made from

cinderblock, it was full of holes and only a few centimetres wide. It was a much tougher challenge than the balance beam in gymnastics. But I was running as fast as a scared kitty can run.

<I'll kill you ALL! FOOLS!> Visser Three screamed.

I hoped he would just forget about me. But then I heard the thunder of his walk. In two steps he had caught up to me.

His huge hand swept towards me.

It was three metres to the ground, and the ground was covered with rusted, twisted metal.

I had no choice. I leaped.

The sharp metal was rushing up at me. Visser Three's hand was sweeping towards me.

Something sharp bit into my back.

The ground was no longer rushing up at me. Instead, I was zooming through the air.

<Jeez, Rachel. Next time you want to morph into a kitty, pick one who doesn't eat so much!>

Tobias!

<I can get you as far as the trees, that's it,> Tobias said.

<I have to morph back,> I said. <My time is up!>

We flew towards the trees. Tobias strained to keep us in the air. I knew he was at his limit of endurance.

<Drop me, now!>

We were in the trees. Tobias dropped me. I fell through the air. But my tail pivoted and kept my balance perfect.

A tree branch! *Slam!* My claws dug into the bark.

I was already morphing back as I dropped to the ground and landed on soft pine needles.

Through the trees I could see the huge beast that was Visser Three rampaging in a fury. The few Hork-Bajir that were left were tossed around like toys. Taxxons were crushed under his feet.

<I think he's mad we got away,> Tobias said.

"Jake? The others?" I demanded. "Did they make it?"

<They're fine. Jake had to morph back into human shape before going into the tiger morph, so he didn't have a problem with the time. Marco got his feathers a little singed, but he's OK. Cassie, too.>

I collapsed on the ground. I had escaped. I had survived. I knew I should have been glad. But all I felt was tired.

Chapter 23

Melissa was at our next gymnastics class. She was still alive. Still free.

I acted nonchalant as I changed into my leotard and stretched out. But I did watch when she opened her locker and pulled out the envelope.

She opened it and read the words I had put there.

"Melissa, your father loves you more than you will ever know. And more than he can ever show you. Signed, someone who knows."

I'd printed it out on my word processor, of course, so she wouldn't recognize my handwriting.

Maybe it was just my imagination, but she seemed more into the practice that day.

After my mum picked me up and drove me

home, I hooked up with the others. We hadn't got together for a couple of days, since the battle at the construction site. I guess I felt like I had some things to think about.

"How is Melissa?" Cassie asked.

I shrugged. "I left her a note." I told them what it had said. "I know it's bad for security, Jake. And Marco, I know it was sentimental. But I don't care. Chapman gave up everything to save his daughter from being made into a host. I had to do something."

Jake nodded. "It's OK. Maybe it will help."

Cassie smiled at me, telling me she was proud of what I'd done. Marco rolled his eyes, but he didn't say anything.

"Well, we destroyed a Yeerk Bug fighter. We made Visser Three nervous. And —"

"— and we came out alive," Marco finished.

"Yeah, that too," Jake agreed with a grin. "That's a very important thing to do."

"Next time we'll —" I began.

"— *next* time?" Marco cried out in mock horror.

<There *will* be a next time,> Tobias said. <There will be a next time until the Andalites return.>

Don't miss . . .

ANIMORPHS

ANIMORPHS 3:

The Encounter

by K.A. Applegate

I wasn't tired any more.

At top speed, I raced back to my friends. I felt sick. I felt like my heart was going to burst.

They had missed the deadline! It was too late. Too late, and they would all be trapped. Like me. Forever.

<MORPH!> I screamed as I closed in on them.

Thought-speak is like regular speech. It gets harder to hear the farther away you are.

<Morph back! Now!> Maybe the clock in the

truck was off. Maybe five minutes one way or the other wouldn't matter.

There! I saw them. Four wolves moving relentlessly toward the distant city.

<Morph! Now!> I screamed as I shot like a bullet over their heads.

<How much time do we have?> Marco demanded.

<None.>

That got them going. I landed, exhausted, on a branch.

Cassie was the first to begin the change. Her fur grew short. Her snout flattened into a nose. Long, human legs swelled and burst from the thin dog legs.

Her tail sucked back in and disappeared. She was already more than half human by the time the first changes began to appear on the others.

<Come on, hurry,> I urged them.

<What time is it?> Jake demanded.

< You have about two minutes,> I said. It was a lie. According to the clock, they were already seven minutes too late.

Too late.

And yet Cassie was continuing to emerge from her wolf body. Skin was replacing fur. Her leotard covered her legs.

<Ahhhh!> I heard Rachel cry in my mind. Her morph was going all wrong. Her human hands

appeared at the end of her wolf legs. But nothing else seemed to be changing.

I looked, horrified, at Marco. His normal head emerged with startling suddenness from his wolf body. But the rest of him had not changed. He looked down at himself and cried out in terror. "Helowl. Yipmeahhh!" It was an awful sound, half human, half wolf.

This was worse than I had feared. I figured they could be trapped as wolves, like I had been trapped as a hawk. But they were emerging as half-human freaks of nature.

They were living nightmares.

And coming soon . . .

ANIMORPHS

ANIMORPHS 4:

The Message

by K.A. Applegate

<You know, I hate to sound like the only sensible person — so to speak — > Tobias said, <but you aren't here to fight sharks!>

<He's right,> I agreed. <Dolphins don't attack sharks unless the sharks attack first.>

<Wait . . . I'm getting more echoes,> Rachel interrupted. <There's more than one shark. And there's something bigger, too.>

I reached out with my echo-location sense and "felt" the sea ahead of me. <You're right,> I said. <Several sharks. And a *great one.*>

<A what?> Tobias asked.

I was confused. What *did* I mean? The words *great one* had just popped into my mind. <I mean there's a *whale*. A whale. Being attacked by sharks.>

<A great one being attacked?> Marco asked. He sounded upset. It was strange, because we were all upset. More than we should have been.

<You guys do what you want,> Rachel said. <I'm going in.>

<Oh, there's a big surprise,> Tobias said with weary affection.

The four of us lanced forward, faster than ever, towards the whale in distress.

We were steaming through the water when I caught sight of my first shark. He was bigger than me, maybe four metres long, with faint vertical stripes.

He was too excited by the hunt to notice me. Until it was too late. With every bit of speed and power I could get from my tail, I rammed the tiger shark in his gill slits.

WHOOOOMP!

It was like hitting a brick wall. My beak was strong, but the shark was made of steel or something.

I fell back, dazed. But as I tried to collect myself I saw that a trail of blood was billowing from the shark's gills.

I swam beneath him, and then I saw the huge

shape of the whale. He was a humpback, more than fifteen metres long. Each one of his long, barnacle-encrusted flukes was bigger than me.

He was trying to surface to breathe, but sharks were attacking, tearing at the soft, vulnerable flesh of his mouth.

It made me angry. Very angry.

Suddenly, from the murky depths, Jake and Rachel zoomed upward, like missiles aimed at the sharks.

WHOOMP! Rachel hit her target.

Jake's shark twisted just in time. Jake scraped across the shark's sandpaper skin, and before he could get clear, the shark was after him.

<Jake! He's on your tail!>

<I got him!>

<Look out! Coming up on your left, Marco!>

They were as fast as we were, as manoeuvrable as we were, and the sharks had one terrifying advantage — they did not know fear.

It was no longer a game. I had gone rushing into a fight full of confidence and determined to help the whale. But now I was in a war. The sharks were killing machines. They seemed to be nothing but armoured skin and razor-sharp fins and wide jaws with row after row of serrated teeth.

The water was boiling with twisting, turning,

speeding sharks and us dolphins, locked in a high-speed battle to the death.

It suddenly occurred to me that we might lose. We might be killed.

<Marco?>

<I . . . I think I'm hurt,> he said.

I looked for him. He was drifting in the water, almost motionless, twenty metres away. We all swam over, crowding around him.

Then I saw the wound. I think I would have screamed, if I could have. His tail had almost been bitten off. It was hanging by a few jagged threads. It was useless.

We were way out in the ocean. And Marco could not hope to swim back. . .

HIPPO GHOST

Ghostly Music
Beth loves her piano lessons. But she's not the
only one interested in them…
Richard Brown

A Patchwork of Ghosts
Who is the evil-looking ghost tormenting Lizzie,
and why does he want to hurt her…?
Angela Bull

The Railway Phantoms
Rachel has visions. She dreams of two children in
strange, disintegrating clothes. And it seems as if
they are trying to contact her…
Dennis Hamley

The Haunting of Gull Cottage
Unless Kezzie and James can find what really
happened in Gull Cottage that terrible night
many years ago, the haunting may never stop…
Tessa Krailing

The Hidden Tomb
Can Kate unlock the mystery of the curse on
Middleton Hall, before it destroys the Mason
family…?
Jenny Oldfield

The House at the End of Ferry Road
The house at the end of Ferry Road has just been
built. So it can't be haunted, can it...?
Martin Oliver

Beware! This House is Haunted
This House is Haunted Too!
Jessica doesn't believe in ghosts. Especially not
ghosts called Beryl who wear school uniform. So
who is writing the spooky notes...?
Lance Salway

The Children Next Door
Laura longs to make friends with the children
next door. When she finally plucks up courage,
she meets Zilla – but she's an only child. So who
are the other children she's seen playing in next
door's garden...?
Jean Ure

And coming soon...

Summer Visitors
Things look up for Emma when she meets the
Carstairs family on the beach. But there's some-
thing very strange about them...
Carol Barton

Reader beware – you choose the scare!

Give Yourself Goosebumps

A scary new series from R.L. Stine – where you decide what happens!

1 Escape From the Carnival of Horrors
2 Tick, Tock, You're Dead!
3 Trapped in Batwing Hall
4 The Deadly Experiment of Dr Eeek

Choose from over 20 scary endings!